# Praise for *Duende*

"This skillful novella, filled with lush and luscious prose, vibrates with energy and passion and keenly observed details, just as does the young narrator's life as she moves through a series of encounters in Sevilla and elsewhere. Smoldering to the sexual heat of flamenco, the story dissects the complicated dynamics of family, love, violence, and growing up, all through author Alex Poppe's unflinching gaze."

—Randall Silvis, author of *When All Light Fails, Disquiet Heart, On Night's Shore, Two Days Gone*, National Endowment for the Arts, Drue Heinz Literature Prize, Fulbright Senior Scholar Research Award, Pennsylvania Council on the Arts

"In this bold and electric contemporary novella, a teenage expat on the cusp of womanhood is caught between two worlds: her childhood home in Detroit where her family's troubled history haunts her, and her year in Seville, where a missing girl populates the periphery of her attention. Suspended by the rhythm of flamenco, Lava, our heroine, is self-reliant by necessity, and her sentimental education examines a body in flux. In intoxicating prose, the intuitive and inventive language of flamenco acts as both a way to keep time and to lose it, as question and answer, as remedy and protest, as forcefield and conduit. In *Duende*, Poppe shows us the links between twin mysteries, how trauma can reverberate through a life, how a girl becomes a woman. This novella is visceral and kinetic; heartbreaking and hopeful, and not one to be missed."

—Kate Wisel, author of *Driving in Cars with Homeless Men*, 2019 Winner of the Drue Heinz Literature Prize

"*Duende* is a remarkable story that dances with electrifying tempo. Pulsing with empathy, lush and sinuous prose taps the soul of flamenco's language. Lava's sense of herself grows with each planta, chaflán, golpe, and we take flight with each page turned. A gifted raconteur, Poppe knows how the world spins."

—Charlie Hailey, author of *The Porch: Meditations on the Edge of Nature, Camp: A Guide to 21st Century Space, and Slab City: Dispatches from the Last Free Place*; Guggenheim Fellow; Fulbright Scholar

"*Duende* reads like Alex Poppe smashed a stained-glass template of the coming-of-age form, then arranged the shards into a brilliant mosaic. It's a spellbinding, unpredictable page-turner, but it is first and foremost an undeniable work of art. When an adolescent American girl in Spain dives headfirst into flamenco, a phantasmagoria of uncompromising truths is churned up, but she refuses to turn back in her pursuit of agency."

—Don De Grazia, author of *American Skin*

"*Duende* is no ordinary coming-of-age tale, although the longing that pulses at its center is as timeless as the flamenco music that weaves through the book. Alex Poppe performs a narrative dance with these pages, weaving together Sevilla, Spain and Detroit, Michigan. Her rhythmic sentences and sensory details will leave you hungering for streetside cafes, flamenco halls, and carnivals. Poppe is a rare storyteller, gifted with both precision and heart."

—Rachel Swearingen, author of *How to Walk on Water and Other Stories*, Winner of the 2018 New American Fiction Prize

"Like the beautiful and complex rhythms of the music of flamenco, Alex Poppe's *Duende* vibrates inside her reader. This moving story explores what it means to be a mother, a daughter, and a woman, and a culture of music and dance provides Lava, the teenaged narrator, a place to belong when belonging is as ephemeral as notes on the breeze. Poppe's exhilarating dance sequences and clear-eyed images of Seville stand in vivid and remarkable contrast to the suffocating grit Lava leaves behind in Detroit, creating a vast and vibrant tapestry of story."

—Patricia Ann McNair, author of *Responsible Adults*, *The Temple of Air*, Chicago Writers Association's Book of the Year, Devil's Kitchen Readers Award, *And These Are The Good Times*, Montaigne Medal finalist

"Alex Poppe's daring and lyrical *Duende* explores teenage sexuality and identity against the contemporary backdrops of Detroit and Seville. Flamenco spirals and enchants through this elegant short novel, leaving you breathless and wanting more."

—Christopher Linforth, author of *The Distortions*, *2020* Orison Books Fiction Prize Winner, and *Directory*

"*Duende* is a hard, rough, ultimately warm loving, revealing story about the world, and the romance of flamenco, of a drug addict and dealer in Detroit, and of a Spanish gypsy he loves, and of her sister, and of Seville, and of a lonely, tough courageous little girl named Lava. Poppe, a rising novelist, can make us cringe, and you feel that she has lived this life, and she can describe it, too, like a lyrical poet. We worry about Lava as she learns, as we all must, that to do something well and to be proud of who you are, that you must struggle, but once you find yourself you become truly alive, and you can dance, and fly on an angel's wing. What young girl doesn't want to fly."

—Jere Van Dyk, author of *The Trade: My Journey into the Labyrinth of Political Kidnapping*, *Captive*, *In Afghanistan: An American Odyssey; The New York Times*, *National Geographic*, CBS News

"Poppe delivers lucid and convincing characters, women and girls who are constantly defined by the way others see them yet refuse to settle within those limitations."

—Jeremy T. Wilson, author of *Adult Teeth*, Nelson Algren Award for Short Fiction Winner

"Lorca wrote that duende is 'a mysterious power that everyone feels and no philosopher can explain...a power, a struggle, that comes from the very soles of the feet.' The animating soul of duende is flamenco at the heart of Poppe's sumptuous novel, which bursts with fervor and pain. Flamenco is the blood, the texture, the passion through which the story speaks. *Duende* is a sensual evocation of a place: Sevilla; of music "like silk unending," of the heat of a body, the flames of a young girl's passion, and her unfolding search for her past in a place that is both far away and home."

—Ellen Kaplan, author of *The Violet Hours, Images of Mental Illness on Stage*

"An absorbing, hard-hitting novella, with nuanced reflections on the families we make for ourselves. The reader will be right there with Alex Poppe, wherever she takes you."

—Stuart Ross, author of *Jenny in Corona*

"With rich prose that is ripe with imagery, author Alex Poppe tells a story filled with the fire of flamenco and the anguish of the yet unknown.

Many authors can tell a character's story in pieces, weaving past and present as the story requires. Lava's story is revealed not so much in pieces as in waves—waves of need and longing and discovery. She tells of people she met and how she met them, introducing us to others because she does not yet know herself. "You will go out into the world many times and be bitten," an old woman tells her. "The important thing is to go out again after you've bled." It is through the bleeding that she discovers her origins. It is through the dance that she discovers who she truly is."

—Cindy Maddox, author of *In the Neighborhood of Normal*

"Such beautiful writing about dance. About pain. About life."

—David Michael Slater, author of *Sparks* and *Fun & Games*

# DUENDE

Alex Poppe

Regal House Publishing

Published by
Regal House Publishing, LLC
Raleigh, NC 27605
All rights reserved

ISBN -13 (paperback): 9781646032419
ISBN -13 (epub): 9781646032426
Library of Congress Control Number: 2021943785

Interior design by Lafayette & Greene
Cover images © by C. B. Royal

Regal House Publishing, LLC
https://regalhousepublishing.com

Printed in the United States of America

For Roberto Reyes
January 2, 1938 – February 16, 2021
*Para carteles y cantos y palmas*
Thank you for showing me your world.

# TANGOS

His name was Daniel Munoz and only for that year in Seville did I know him. His family owned a *bodegita* near the language school where Lola, my mother's cousin, enrolled me after I'd been sent to live with her. Lola lived in a trinity house, all narrow halls and steep steps, close to the river, and in the bluish mornings, guitar music would lilt down from the windows and float through the *callejones* toward the *gitano* quarter of Triana, where flamenco was born. Sometimes, Lola would stop what she was doing to dance. Her twig-like fingers latticed the air, tiny drops of sweat running in rivulets down her wrists. Eyes closed, back spiraling, she'd sculpt mermaid shapes out of air, keeping time with the hinge of her jaw. When the music pulsed with urgency, Lola's feet stamped with chaos before crashing onto a wave of silence. Lola danced flamenco the way she lived. Every floor in the house was scarred with abandon.

I arrived in early summer when the air was fragrant with orange blossom and lilac, and the Andalusian sun made everything soft and gleaming and implausible. The *barrio* where Lola lived was a tangle of narrow cobbled streets anchored by *albacerias*, and in the early mornings, a soft wave of voices murmured beneath the rustle of newspapers as locals enjoyed a second breakfast in the wood paneled cafes strung with cuts of pork, for in Seville, life was lived *en la calle*, and any opportunity to socialize was seized with relish. To the chime of china, I'd unlock my rented bike and pedal to Plaza de la Alfalfa, outlined by family-run, neighborhood businesses competing with new venture start-ups, to spend my mornings conjugating verbs and wondering how the side roads of life had taken me from Detroit to here. It was 2015, the year my father returned, and our boarder, Cody, left, and everything changed. I was sixteen—quiet, desperate to be reckless, and impatient to enter adulthood.

Daniel was fair for a Spaniard, his mouth a red surprise in his pale face. Having one American-born parent, he spoke English, which brokered a friendship between us. Daniel was seventeen, about to start his last year of high school, and longed to go to America for college. Most afternoons after my Spanish class, I'd walk across the plaza to Bodeguita Fabiola to snack at the bar, and Daniel and I'd talk about American films as he served customers. When he got busy, his four octave *claro que sí*, bellowed in response to a customer request, vibrated across the bar to step up the ladder of my chest. His accent lent a musicality to his spoken English, a richness of bass underscoring a euphony of melody that made my ears greedy. When someone proposed something he didn't like, a multiple no, ("No, no, nope, uh-uh no!"), fell from his lips as he wagged his head from side to side. By the time the lunch rush was over, Daniel's mutinous curls would have broken free from the confines of hair gel. Brushing aside a flop of sloppy whorls, he'd flash me a wide smile and turn his back to down a self-congratulatory *caña* of beer, "training," he called it for his future fraternity life in the States. If he didn't go to the US, Daniel hoped to travel Asia or at least leave Andalusia. He scorned flamenco, bull fighting, and *tabernas* as old-fashioned, preferring the slick craft beer pubs which sprouted along the Alameda, a poplar tree-lined avenue trimmed by cafes and fusion restaurants. He'd lean across the bar to correct my Spanish homework, his candied breath warm in my ear, and I'd confuse the grammatical state of being just so he could explain it again. "*Estar* (to be) describes something temporary," he'd say, mischief scrambling his facial features. "*Estoy piripi*," (I am tipsy), and he'd pratfall over the bar, grabbing my shoulders for support. Electric bolts jigged up and down my arms long after he'd removed his hands. "*Ser* (to be) is used for something permanent," he leaned in close enough to kiss. "*Tu sonrisa es muy bonita*," (Your smile is very pretty), the charmer in him seeking the limelight. He flirted with everyone: to be in the spotlight of his attention made a person feel seen. Sometimes, older women would come in, some old enough to have birthed him, and discreetly leave a key wrapped in a note beneath a crumpled napkin, their *tapa de tortilla Española* barely touched. Without looking, Daniel would palm the key into his pocket as he skimmed the note and then adjusted himself. Many of these women were tourists who filled the Airbnbs that flowered the neighborhood, women who happened upon Fabiola's, sweat water-coloring their made-up faces, and found reason, in the accommodating young barman, to return; others were locals, women who spoke the clipped accent of Seville, their starving eyes helping themselves to Daniel's view. Between five p.m. and eight p.m., when most restaurants and cafes closed for *siesta*, Daniel would follow his day's selection to a hushed room with drawn blinds and cool sheets and be instructed in the art of sex. We never talked about his leggy pursuits, although some of the women who came for him made small talk with me with their thick and ugly tongues, painting me into their scene. When his shift ended, Daniel would disappear into the labyrinth of streets as I unlocked my bicycle and pedaled back to Lola's or to the *taller* where she gave classes.

Lola taught me flamenco's language; basic *zapateados* which transformed my heels and toes into the sound of a warring army, *braceos*, where my arms became swans, flower-like hand movements that origamied the air and articulated finger pulses to punctuate them, hip rocks which saturated flamenco with sensuality, and poses that imbued the dancer with insouciance. These movements, the words of flamenco, formed its linguistic structure, which was what enabled dancers, guitarists, and singers to play together when they first met. Only after a performer became fluent in flamenco's structure could he create new movements, "words," to allow for personal expression. This was flamenco's magic: a primal, improvised interpretation built upon a common past which transcended spoken language, an immediate yet fleeting shared creation—*duende*.

When Lola danced, she was *empapado en música*, drenched in music, in feeling, in moment. This is what riveted eyes to her, for music dwelt in Lola's vociferous, perishable body, and flamenco was its protest. *Danzaora. Sevillana. Creator. Woman.* The words bellowed with every percussive strike of Lola's heels. Other words, *Impure, Bold, Shameless,* rustled under the brushes of Lola's toe tip. An ecstasy of stamps. *Unstoppable.* When Lola danced *a palo seco,* without accompaniment, flamenco embraced the avant-garde. She'd rock her upper body like a metronome before her feet beat the rhythm into triple time. Snapping fingers slowed the percussion down to silence as Lola's body swanned and then held itself in arabesque, fluid in its suspension. When her outstretched leg swung forward, it changed the cadence of the dance. Arms vulcanning behind her head, they undulated as if conjuring spirits from the underworld, and her body went from firecracker to flare. Her head became the fulcrum of movement, a point of origin for the fervent turns that corkscrewed her body. With a leap, she was dancing on her back, slow-motion twists and turns of her wrists and feet marking the time, her legs writhing in the air, the body's secrets come to light. This dance announced, *Yo soy.* I am.

"*Flamenco es fuerte,*" Lola shouted as she clapped the 3/4 rhythm of the *soleá.* I was struggling with all my moving parts: keeping different rhythms with my hands and feet at the same time confused me. "Stop thinking," she'd yell in Spanish. "Feel," for dancing flamenco without feeling any emotion ignored the dance's soul. In Lola's studio, with the mirror throwing a reflection, my arms became snakes as one foot slid forward, and the other stamped the floor. "Show me what you're made of," Lola dared. Pictures flashed on the scrim of my mind: glass shards from a crack pipe being picked from the heel of my four-year-old foot; a mouth like a guppy's bringing a sloppy kiss toward my ducking lips; dark asphalt falling away as a plane gained on the aging day, and I filled with an untamed feeling, a screaming note all through me. I exploded with sound: my heels striking in *doble tiempo* while my hands slapped the *contratiempo* across my upper thighs. "*Alé,*" Lola shouted in encouragement. Moisture collected in my eyes as my feet took over, a fever of movement, my legs praying. I danced a *remate* to close the phrase of extended footwork. A moment of calm. There was a conversation in the silence that my arm carried as it circled above my head and then down, fingers moving like eyelashes, until I was leaning back into an unseen partner. Over my own smell, Daniel's cologne surfed the air. I leaned farther until my hands met the floor, my body star-fished, and then settled into a series of waves. Undulating, I beat the rhythm into the floor with my fist before pulling myself to standing, finger snaps taking the tempo, my hips following. Instead of rocking my hips from side to side as female dancers traditionally did, I shook mine forward and back like a man and then mixed the two as I strutted my way off stage. These movements were my first words in flamenco: *me voy convirtiendo*. I am becoming.

Each summer morning, the sun rose, bleeding warmth onto the rooftops, building in intensity like the *compás* of a *bulería* until everything ate the light. Later, coated in a salty residue of sweat, Daniel and I would sit at the bar and watch the news as July wore on, and the flow of afternoon customers dwindled. We were consumed with the story of a local girl from a prominent family, missing since the Seville Fair that April, lost in a frisson of dancing and drinking and expected to turn up, passed out in one of the horse-drawn carriages parading the fairgrounds. Guests at the family's *caseta*, fine women and men playing at being young again while their sons and daughters stood around ice buckets of beer bottles and played at being old, were interviewed, and then the bartenders and doormen, and finally, a call went out to the general public. The story fell from the headlines as a steady stream of refugees making their way toward Europe captured international attention, but it re-captivated local *Sevillanos* when the girl's body was found in a well near a town famous for its vineyards.

Daniel was garnishing a plate of honey-drizzled goat cheese with walnuts and sliced dried apricots when a news bulletin interrupted the local soap opera he insisted I watch to improve my Spanish. "*Ella está muerta,*" proclaimed the news announcer, her face grave behind a mask of Botox.

"I knew it," Daniel proclaimed, the knife he was holding an exclamation point in the air. He stopped cutting to retrieve the remote and turned up the volume.

"What's she saying?" The announcer's Spanish was too fast me for me to follow.

"Shhhhh." Daniel was transfixed, nodding his head from time to time as the story unraveled. I pictured a pale girl floating in dark water, twigs and leaves tangled in the spider web of her hair, the ruffles on her flamenco dress sleeves fanning out, the flounce of her skirt fishtailing her legs.

"That's near my grandfather's bodega!" he said. When the television station cut to a commercial, Daniel placed the plate of goat cheese and a basket of bread between us and poured two *cañas* of beer.

"What is?" My back blossomed with goose bumps as he touched a beer to my neck.

"Trebujena, the town where they found the body."

"Tell me everything." I tore a hunk of bread from the loaf and handed it to Daniel, bits of crust snow-flaking the bar. He spread it with goat cheese and honey, folding in some nuts and fruit, took a few large, unapologetic bites, and handed it back to me. I passed him another chunk of bread.

"The well is on the property of an old whorehouse that people sometimes use for parties."

"What?"

The front door opened blasting us with heat. Two pasty British tourists lobstered by the sun entered and sat at the far end of the bar. I waited for Daniel to serve them.

"Old whores need other ways to make money. Their house is on the outskirts of town, so it's perfect for raves."

"Have you been to one?"

Daniel flashed me a look, his eyes two bright tunnels. "The body was found when repairs were being done to the septic system. None of the old whores know how it got there." He drank some beer, his pistoning Adam's apple stopping mid-swallow, an elevator stuck between two floors. "Wait. Those old whores have been drinking dead-girl water."

I put down my sandwich. "Do the police know who did it?"

"No. The last time anyone saw her was at the *feria*. The killer could be right here in Sevilla." His voice got scratchier as his arms monstered above his head, elbows out and back, the elegance of a natural flamenco. "Be afraid, be very, very afraid."

"Shut up." My fingertips lingered on his chest before pushing him away.

Daniel went to check on his customers. Above the bar, the news footage showed an old windowless stone house surrounded by hard land. A whitewashed well stood adjacent, garlanded by hoary weeds while in the distance, rows of vines conquered the desolate soil. A phantom wind animated a scattering of overgrown grass. In my head, I heard the soft rushes of a dancer's foot sliding along gravel and saw the not-yet-drowned girl being dragged along a packed dirt path toward the well. Heels stamping the ground in a furious rhythm, they fail to make purchase before her body is hoisted onto the well's lip. A frenzy of footwork as she is thrust backwards, cracking her head on the stone basin, her limbs quiet yet riotous, as she falls into darkness.

"Are you okay?" Daniel wiped his hands with a bar rag.

I shook a shadow from my shoulder. "Hey, why do they say '*está muerta*'? Shouldn't it be '*es muerta*'?" My eyes flicked to the TV, where a smiling picture of the dead girl dwarfed the newscaster's head.

"Yee American, we Spaniards do not think of death as permanent. *Volvimos*, we return. Our souls get reborn or something."

I rested my chin on my hands as Daniel greeted a new customer. Was that dead girl's soul trapped inside the well, waiting for a chance to return? Or had it sunk deeper inside her, barricading itself behind deteriorating flesh and connective tissue, shrinking into deeper and deeper recesses until it was so far gone as to be lost forever?

❦

With August came the blinding heat that drove *Sevillanos* to seek refuge on the beaches surrounding Portugal and Spain. Daniel's family shuttered their *bodeguita* and headed north to Asturias. My language school also closed, and I spent my days in Lola's studio learning the *farruca*, a melancholic, virile, deliberate dance whose severe attitudes and quick, intense footwork absorbed my longing. Because the *farruca* was traditionally performed by men, Lola allowed me to practice in jeans, my body's center lowering, chest lifting, hips still. With its dramatic shifts in tempo, the *farruca* allowed for interpretation. There was graceful phrasing filled with lunge-like steps and soundless turns. Liquid movement gave way to heel stamping *subidas*, to increase the tempo, punctuated with sharp poses and long *escobillas* to show off the dancer's footwork, and ended with a *llamada* or a call which invited the guitarist to slow the rhythm back to its original tempo. Over intricate guitar improvisations, my arms took the focus of movement, affording me a playfulness that mimicked Daniel's charisma and led me through a series of turns that covered the length of the studio's floor. Dancing the *farruca's* molten sequences, taking space, I was emboldened. I'd leave the studio and swagger my way home, stopping to test drive my fledgling Spanish on shop keepers re-opening for business after the day's *siesta*.

In September, Lola enrolled me in a secondary school, and I didn't see Daniel, for he too went back to *colegio*, having traded hedonistic misdemeanors for the mind bend of *Bachillerato* preparation. When another dead girl turned up in the marshy lowlands of the Guadalquivir River, I made my way under the wide arc of the sky toward Fabiola's. Daniel was sitting at an outside table, legs sprawled, the nexus of his group. Scattered around the plaza, tabletop candles winked on and off like drifting embers. In the shadow of an old church, I stood very still, counting the *farruca's* 4/4 rhythm, conjuring the butterfly fluttering of guitar strings. My arms rose to third position, my chest arching up and out, my feet gliding forward as my arms returned to my sides. I neared his group.

"I thought I'd see you tonight." Daniel's curls, lionized by the summer sun, had grown longer; he wore them tied back at the crown of his head.

"You return from vacation, and another girl turns up dead. Coincidence?"

Daniel creepified his voice. "Be afraid. Be very, very afraid." His voice returned to normal as he switched to Spanish. "Everyone, this is Lava. Lava, this is, well, everyone."

In my head, my feet were accenting the one, three, five, and seven beats of the *farruca's* double measures while my fingers made fanning movements behind my back. I gave a smile to the conga line of faces.

"Come on. Let's get you a *caña*." Daniel grabbed my hand and led me inside Fabiola's. His palms wore a dress of sweat. We sidled up to the bar and got walled in by people. "How was the rest of your summer?"

The heartbeat of *tacón* steps echoed in my head. "Good." Flamenco, with its language of violence and romance, had tempered my boredom and impatience. "I was with my cousin a lot. How was Asturias?"

"Fun." The corners of Daniel's mouth gimped upwards. "Lots of tourists." He looked at me as if to figure out how tall I was. "You seem different." Above his upper lip, a thin sheen of sweat played hide-and-seek with the bar light.

"Different how?"

"I don't know. Like you, but more."

People swelled toward the bar, pushing me into Daniel.

"Sorry," I said, stepping on his sandaled feet.

He righted me. "Your giggles are brimming with sympathy." He feigned pain. "Ow. I think my toes are broken. Ow! And now my arm is too."

"I didn't hit you that hard. This time anyway."

"I see. The lady's got a lust for violence. Maybe you're the killer dumping vulnerable young girls in the scenic panorama of Andalusia."

"Maybe." We clanked glasses and drank. "We're all possible killers."

"I don't believe that." He stifled a burp.

I did. "Look at soldiers and police officers. They don't think 'Hmm. I think I want to kill someone. I know! I'll join the force,' but then they do."

"They kill because of their jobs. They have to."

"That's my point. We are all possible killers. And police don't always have to. You've heard of 'Hands up, don't shoot.'?"

"That's America."

"What about accidental killers like drunk drivers? Or un-witting killers like drug dealers whose clients OD? Or even better, the self-glorified disillusioned who shoot up schools and churches."

"Those are extremes, and America, and not people generally."

Siren lights spun in my funhouse mirror of memory. "Drug addicts, not nationality specific, who do terrible things because they need a fix."

"That's very specific. Do you know anyone that's actually happened to?"

I held my glass of beer to my heating face. "How about people who kill to protect their families?"

"Again, how often does that happen?"

"But it does, and that's my point. All of us are possibly violent, maybe even to the point of murder."

"Okay, under what circumstances could you kill?"

"Rage." I sipped at my beer. "What's so funny?"

"You say 'rage' so calmly. I might—for love."

"That is so cliché, not to mention contradictory."

"Says the raging teen. How so?"

"Love is supposed to be benevolent, sometime redemptive, but violent?"

"You said it yourself. Someone is protecting his family, the people he loves."

"Maybe protecting them is about ego, to be the hero. Or maybe it's something instinctual, so there's no before thought. It could also be a sense of duty. But none of those motives are love."

"Crimes of passion?"

"Passion isn't love. It's like fake bacon. It's mock love."

"Fake meat is good food." Daniel gave me his big eyes.

Our conversation lulled as we got lost in a staring-contest moment.

Daniel finished his beer. "So."

"So." I served the word back to him.

Daniel eyed the crowd. "It's hot here. Wanna go by the river?"

"Okay."

Daniel's hand slithered along my waist, leading me through a sea of patrons. Along the plaza, café tables spilled with people as if the city's streets had magnetized all of Seville from their homes. I breathed deeply. The faint smell of verbena underscored a perfume of jasmine and rose teasing the dry night air. Cigarette smoke from a nearby table laced the sweetness, panthering it like the stealthy *compás* beneath a flamenco guitar melody. When I snagged Daniel's eye, the entire canon of flamenco's emotions compressed like a rope of rainbow-colored scarves into a magician's pocket.

He weaved us through a knot of narrow streets toward the Guadalquivir, where the river had turned a milky pewter. We walked down some steps to the embankment and followed the water under the guard of stars. The memory carousel in my mind spun images of splayed insulation and crusted, discarded socks littering the overgrown lawns of my Detroit neighborhood, derelict houses fingering their way onto our block, their glassless windows like phantom eyes tracking my every move. Here was the gentle laughter of the river echoing off an embankment lined by pastel-hued houses, and the faint strum of guitar music to accompany our walk. When Daniel pulled me close and kissed me by the river's edge, I was mystified by the luck of life.

That first kiss begot another and then another like beads on a string. The inside of Daniel's mouth was a racetrack full of dangerous curves. I ran slick. We found a bench where we lost our hands in each other's clothes. I was on my back, and he was on my front, and I thought about saying stop when the *farruca*, with its urgent rage and beauty, pulsed through me, sparking something wild, something vivid. In my head echoed a stampeding *escobilla*, building in rhythm to rival Daniel's breathing, until he was on his back, and I was on his front, astride and confused as to what to do. My heart beat between my legs. Like learning flamenco, I stopped thinking and let myself feel as my world condensed to a spear of pain which melded into warm, elastic wetness. My hips rocked back and forth, finding Daniel's rhythm, finding their way. Behind my eyelids were swirls of color: the iris, orange, and yellow of sunset, now a twirling flamenco skirt. I was spinning to crescendo, an ecstatic furor which climaxed with an arm raised in triumph, a wild breathless second cut short as Daniel pulled out and came. As our rhythm collapsed, I slipped from the park bench, catching myself on one knee as Daniel stilled, exertion coloring his cheeks, his bared teeth fixed in a grimace of animal taxidermy, eyelids twitching. I was desperate for a mirror, for I wanted to see if I looked different too.

"Do you have a tissue?" Daniel's hips jostled, his body turning indifferent.

He was blood stained, the remnants of a burnt-out fire. "Let me check." Swinging my leg around, I unsaddled him and knelt beside the bench, pressing my thighs together as I rummaged through my bag. "Here."

He took a Kleenex from the pack. "Thanks," he said, and wiped himself. "I didn't think it'd be your first time."

"Why not?" I took a Kleenex too.

"You're American."

"You're funny." I turned away to clean myself, thankful for the cobalt dark. There was a constellation of blood on the hem of my skirt, which I hid under my knee. "Is that okay?"

"I guess." He threw our tissues toward the river. They caught on the concrete lip of the causeway before a gust of river breeze turned them into tumbleweeds.

A moment before, we had been interlocking puzzle pieces; now only the ghost heat remained. I stood, arms and chest moving in slow-motion stateliness, while the drilling ferocity of my heels went from mischief to murder in the space of a phrase.

"You are full of surprises," said Daniel, his eyes on my feet.

Flamenco is decision-making with no regrets. I sat back down and pulled him close, pecking his salty, linty neck, inhaling his scent of musk and mollusks. "Don't worry. I won't get obsessed because you were my first."

Daniel looked dubious, the man he was not yet, twinning beneath the child he used to be.

Tilting back my head, I promised the unfeeling stars. "Not even a little." A tear slid from eye to ear. I stood. "I should go."

"I'll walk you."

"It's okay. I know the way."

"We're going the same direction."

Morning twilight broke as we approached the street in our own circles of silence. A beat started as a wiggle in my shoulders, tremoring through my torso until it lodged in my hips, flower-bulbing my body. Swaying to my own rhythm, I turned to Daniel, my right hand twisting up, index and middle fingers touching my right temple and then away. My feet followed, striding into a world that was black and blue and made of outlines.

# LAS SEVILLANAS

Her name was Astrid Molinas and only for that year in Seville did I know her. This was at Colegio International San Francisco de Paula, the Catholic high school where my mother's cousin Lola enrolled me after I had been sent to live with her. I arrived in late May, when the daylight sky was a pure, crisp, sun-soaked blue, aldelfa and jacaranda trees shooting fireworks of pink and purple against its candied scrim. I spent most of the summer taking Spanish classes at a local language academy filled with vacationing foreigners or with Lola in her dance studio learning the language of flamenco. September brought me back to the world of teenagers, and I struggled to be as carefree as they were, unscarred by life's ambushes lying in wait. The expat kids cliqued off together, joining the same clubs, eating lunch at the same table, forming an exclusive WhatsApp group. Their leader was Astrid, a German with a charmingly ugly haircut, who sat next to me in biology. On the second day of the semester, our teacher Señor Aguayo, with his slouchy, science-teacher posture, stood at her desk, resting his scrotum on the corner of it. Astrid remained very calm, listening like a foreigner who needs directions repeated, as hushed giggles rusted her face. Early the next day, she snuck into the classroom to wipe the corner of her desk with a dirty chalkboard eraser. The next time Señor Aguayo settled himself in front of her, he walked away with a white powdered pants front. It was 2015, the year a millionaire TV host decided to run for president, and the people in a poor city near my own were poisoned by lead in their drinking water. It was the year I stopped believing in anything, the year being around my family made me feel alone. The year a three-year-old washed up on a beach, struggling to reach Europe, and my mother sent me there just because. I was sixteen, simmering and unsettled, and in awe of a skinny girl with European teeth and lopsided hair.

I was waiting for Astrid outside the principal's office, pulling threads of her voice from beyond the door frame. When she came out, she gave me a pigeon's stare. "Was it bad?" I addressed her in English.

She blinked as if trailing a blanket of daydreams and then shook her head, giving herself a private smile. "So worth it."

"It was so cool."

"Not when he first did it. Vomit was percolating in the back of my throat."

"You couldn't tell."

"Way. I wanted to bleach my brain but then," she grinned, revealing a snaggle tooth, "I thought of something better."

I choked back laughter. "Sorry. When I think of his sugar-frosted—" I cupped a hand between my upper thighs.

"Nut sack."

"Balls."

"Love spuds."

I snorted. "Goolies."

"Nuggets."

We succumbed to an attack of punishable giggles.

"Stop. My sides hurt." I wiped my eyes.

"Yeah. No." Astrid swallowed hard, her laugh, dark and liquid. The Saint Christopher medal around her neck hooked some sunlight, which sparked in the trophy case beside her. "Nice to know some things are the same in every culture."

"Like fart humor."

"Air biscuit."

"Ass blast."

"Anal salute."

"Fancy." I cocked her an eyebrow. "Anal audio."

"Anal exhale."

"Anal acoustics."

"Anal applause." Astrid let one rip.

"Hahahahahahaha."

I leaned against the hallway wall to catch my breath.
"Farting is underrated." Astrid wafted her stank in my direction. "It's really a bonding experience." She side-eyed me. "I think we're going to be friends."

"Is it safe to breathe?"

Astrid took a gigantic inhale. "Like perfume." She flared her nostrils. "I'm Astrid."

"I know. Lava."

"American?"

I nodded.

"You don't seem American."

"How come?"

"You're not fiercely smiling."

"Why is your English so good?"

"My dad works in international development. I've lived *everywhere*." Astrid let out a theatrical groan as we approached the cafeteria. "UGHH. Do you smell that? It's like, like sandwich meat and unwashed hair, and I don't know, glue?" She tucked her nose into her shoulder until we cleared the doorway. "Man, the world is always sixty to seventy percent slimier than I expect."

"It's one long con."

"Yeah." She turned to me in recognition. "Yeah."

We arrived at the bike racks inside the school gates. "This is me." I stopped at my Sevici bike rental.

"Those handle bars look like a pelvic diagram." She flicked me a look. "How long have you been here?"

My mind flashed to summer: the sky, fiery carnation against the river, livid thistle overhead; flamenco music washing over me like silk unending. The slat surface of a park bench stenciling my thighs as my gut filled with humming birds and raspberry jam. The violent hiccup of Daniel's withdrawal, his sex streaked with him and me, all around us, a silence the color of urban snowfall. I repacked the image and put it back on a corner shelf in my mind. From the ground, a piece of chewed gum drew my eye, and I was overwhelmed by the urge to box a 4/4 rhythm into the bike rack. Instead, I concentrated on the *farruca's* steady *compás*, letting it pulse inside me, guitar notes like licks of moonlight dancing upon river water, until my stomach released. "A few months."

"Whoa. You were here when they found that girl's body in the well."

"Yeah."

"What happened? Did the town go nuts?"

"I guess. It was on TV a lot. Where were you?"

"Lake Wannsee. My family has a summer house there."

A car horn bleated from beyond the school's gate.

"That's me." Astrid handed me her phone. "Here. Give me your number so I can add you to our WhatsApp group," and then waved in the direction of a dark gray Audi. "Can't wait to tell my dad about detention."

"Will you get into a lot of trouble?" I handed her back her phone.

"Thanks. Are you kidding? They'll probably take me out to dinner for this. See you tomorrow." She skipped toward the car as the figure behind the steering wheel stretched across the front seat to open the door for her. As she got inside, a man's open hand reached for her hair, and I imagined her "Whoa" or "Way" sliding in both directions as she dodged it. I unlocked my bike and road toward Lola's studio.

"*Tú estas tarde,*" Lola was tapping a thick wooden stick against the floor to accentuate the *compás* of the *palo* as I snuck into the practice room.

"*Lo siento. He hecho una amiga.*" I hoped my making a friend would please her.

She nodded to a pile of practice wrap skirts on the floor. I took a piece of cloth and tied it around my waist before joining a line of dancers sweating in the windowless room. My *desplantes*, the strong stamps used to mark a sequence's climax, were thick and slow, imprecise with inexperience.

"*Feo,*" Lola's "ugly" was a splinter of glass.

I took refuge on a chair in the corner of the rehearsal room, my T-shirt pulled up over my nose. Sitting, my feet sought the ground as my arms stretched skyward, a thumb on each hand clicking against a middle finger, my diaphragm contracting and expanding before my feet stamped the life force of the *palo's* verse into the floor, the raucous of a thousand cell doors closing. I stood, a broke-back tree righting itself, and rejoined the mass of bodies extending up, arms skyward in preparation for the tirade of foot stamps to follow. The rhythm, tenacious and propulsive and narcotic, transported me to a fall of warring hail during Detroit spring, a strobing red/blue light bruising the matte darkness, a retreating figure blurring in and out of focus like a rapidly striking flamenco heel against a hard wood floor.

"*Agua,*" Lola shouted, and I came back to myself, my feet promptly tangling like hangers. Ripping off the rehearsal skirt, I grabbed my things and scrammed, biking over the Triana Bridge, fleeing the hazing chill brushing the river.

Back home, flamenco music lilted like laughter from the rooftop where Lola's father, Roberto, sat, limbering his fingers along guitar strings in the peach-colored light. Roberto, a flamenco *gitano* from *el campo*, lived in an apartment addition above my bedroom. Often, as I was waking for my school day, I'd hear the slow ascent of uneven steps, a guitar case bumping against a stairwell wall, and then a shuffle across my ceiling as Roberto made his way into bed, and I made my way out, my bladder as tight as a fist, the sun cresting on a distant church steeple. He'd awaken sometime in the afternoon, with the rest of the *Sevillanos* rebooting from their afternoon *siestas*, and take to the rooftop to play the songs of his childhood, his guitar a conduit for the *sentimientos fuertes* that fueled flamenco, for flamenco's *palos* were borne in a hearth of heartbreak and longing. I'd go quiet with listening as his limbered fingers made my heart feel as though it were running through a field. Today, he was playing the *guajira*. With my rooftop appearance his strumming slowed, issuing a *llamada*, an invitation for me to enter the *canción*. My right arm swept a large circle, pausing at twelve o'clock, hand turned toward my face, thumb and middle finger touching. Like a wing, my arm beat inward before the toe of my shoe stamped a four count, revving an internal engine. My leg became a prancing horse's, the ball of my foot lapping at the rooftop. Executing a swift half turn, I arched from my middle back, hips rocking from side to side, hands clapping above my head, and transformed into a toreador. The song was my bull, and I was determined to master it. I turned again, my hands flowering, before they gave way to the silent language of my fingers, each joint articulating the odyssey of living. A lunge right set up a series of chest turns which transported me across the red clay roof until I was dancing at its edge. Under a blue canopy of sky, I stamped the day's frustration into the rooftop. Roberto stopped playing, keeping the *compás* through clapping, eyes glued to my feet, letting me discover new shapes, new words, to add to my flamenco vocabulary aloft the safety net of his percussion. My arms elongated into spears, pinwheeling on either side of my head. Lifted on a breath of wind, I was a phoenix taking flight, soaring over Mudéjar palaces, clearing church steeples, swooping down to the Guadalquivir River, following along the marshy scrub grass of the Doñana wetlands to the Atlantic Ocean, roiling, rollicking, free. I pirouetted to Roberto, bending at one knee, and rested my head in the curve of his guitar. My eyes sought his as we swam on a comet's tail of ineffable memory. A palimpsest of rhythms— African, Caribbean, Andalusian, and Castilian, asterisked then stilled. In that hush was the life of a flamenco: in the silence and the songs and the *campo* and the caves and the cliffs.

"*Alé,*" Robert's eyes were as inky as trees when night falls.

"*Codos hacia afuera,*" Lola broke the awe of the moment.

"I know." I threw the words at her from under my breath even I as took her advice and turned my elbows out. Roberto, lost in some faraway place, said nothing. Being with them both was a bit like trying on someone else's glasses, a bit like confronting an angry wasp, a bit like standing on the edge of a black hole, its gravity pulling you in. I removed my head from Roberto's guitar and sought the door which led to the freeze-dry of the house.

"*Juega para mi, Papá.*" Lola's voice had something hard at the bottom.

Hand on handle, I paused, having never seen them perform together.

Roberto began with a *siguiriya*. Instead of entering slowly as is traditionally done, Lola attacked the song's *letra* with driving footwork, culminating in a dramatic *remate* to close the phrase. Roberto stayed with her, his eyes bouncing between her face and feet, his heart breaking through his fingers, his expectation battling his pride as he improvised the *falseta*, and then issued a *llamada*, to me? As he held an A chord, plucking the *palo's* rhythmic pulse, I entered, keeping Lola at the center of attention, unsure if the invitation was shared by both, letting Lola dictate the *letra's* mood, tempo, and content. Her hands, palms open to the fading sun, rose on fully elongated arms and with a quick twist turned into serpents encouraged by Roberto's impellent rhythm. She smiled, and then seemed to change her mind, cutting her back to me, her arms outstretched as in crucifixion, and gave a face full of anguish to Roberto, who internalized her tragedy and served it back as his own. Their force field was palpable, a magnetic repulsion that threatened the earth's rotation upon its axis. I improvised a *cierre* toward the door.

Lola spiraled as the rhythm softened, remarking that this was the second time that day I was leaving her dance floor. She introduced a *subida* to increase the tempo, which Roberto's guitar followed, and danced a loud *escobilla* to drown out any potential response. She was still punishing the rooftop when I entered my bedroom.

Lying on the bed, I watched the ceiling, half expecting Lola's foot to drive through it, wishing I could put Roberto, Lola, and me on a virtual reality triptych, so we could decode one another's minds. I was unsure how much explanation had accompanied my arrival on Cousin Lola's doorstep and couldn't decipher the Spanish torn by static that crisped over the 4G network from my mother's mouth in Detroit to Lola's ear here.

A WhatsApp message from Astrid yanked me from the labyrinth of speculation. She had added me to her group and was inviting me to a coffee house on the Alameda where some of us would drink caramel lattes, and others would drink craft beer, and everyone would try on a persona of someone he thought he might become. I scribbled Lola a note and traded the pathos of flamenco for the drama of adolescence and made my way to the poplar-lined avenue, banked by coffee houses and bars, to inhabit the IRL of teenagers for a while.

"I'm glad you could make it," Astrid kissed me on both cheeks as I went in for a quick hug; our initial liking of each other an unripe avocado: real but not ready.

"Thanks for the invite. In the nick of time."

"Why? What happened?"

"Stupid stuff. Let me get something." I ordered a café bonbon to soothe my emotional hangover.

From the corner of the café came the slow strum of a *soleá*.

"Why does the beginning of every flamenco song sound like an espresso commercial?" Astrid contorted her face and began braying.

"Are you…singing?" A few heads turned in her direction.

Astrid twirled around me like a drunk toddler. "I'm flamencking." She swiveled her hips as if hula dancing.

"So, you're not a flamenco fan?"

"You are?"

"It's okay." I crossed my fingers behind my back.

"I hate that we have a *sevillanas* class at school. It's a GPA buster. And talk about home-court advantage. It's not like we grow up with the rhythms."

My mind flashed to a photograph on Lola's living room mantel. In it, Lola, buxom and lupine, sits in a circle of women, a baby sleeping on its belly in her lap, while she claps the *palmas* above its head. Other women hold babies too, some sleeping, some sitting upright against their mothers' bellies, feeling the heartbeat of the rhythm reverberate against their backs, saucer eyes watching, heads bobbling, tiny hands bumping into each other to make sound. "If you promise not to judge me, I will help you with the *sevillanas.*"

"How do you know the dance? You moved here like a minute ago."

I flashed to the hot hours spent in Lola's studio. "My cousin taught me."

"It's such a stupid dance. It's a lot of walking forward and back while you wave your arms to keep the music off your face and slide past your partner as he tries to cop a feel."

"The set steps make it easier to learn." Unlike other dances in flamenco, the *sevillanas* was not improvised.

"If I didn't know better, I'd think you were a closeted lover."

Betraying myself for someone else's favor, I lied. "Not really."

"It's okay if you like flamenco. I'll still be your friend."

"That's big of you."

Astrid curtsied, wobbling in her Doc Marten combat boots. "I'm not sure how the others will feel," she said, and then popped back up, her internal velocity that of a pinball in play. "Why did your family move to Seville?"

There was the ghost echo of angry voices, accusations, tears. I decided to stitch up her assumption. "Why not? It's a nice place."

"Too small. Give me Berlin or Paris any day."

From the palace of memory, an image whizzed by of a knife sticking in my arm. "I think they were ready for a change." I tried on lying and found it fit. "Plus, my mom missed her culture."

"Was she born here?"

"Yes, but her family moved to the US when she was a baby. She used to spend her summers here when she was young." Outside the café, flamenco stamps were Morse coding. "But what about you? It seems like you've lived in a lot of cool places."

"Yeah. It's good practice for when I take over the world."

"What's first on your To-Do list?"

"Abolishing the *sevillanas.*"

Sometimes, laughter felt like dancing. "Partner with me tomorrow. We'll figure it out."

When I returned to Lola's, the house was dark. Roberto was out, probably playing guitar in some *taberna* in La Macarena, a working-class neighborhood now hip with artists. I had followed him once to an old dive where he sat among beer kegs playing guitar for the orange wine-soaked locals who danced flamenco barefoot on the worn tile floor. As the hours tangled, singers gathered, improvising the *palos* they had grown up with, an archipelago of shared memories, and I wondered why I never saw Roberto talk to his daughter. Lola was gone too. I lay listening to the silence of an empty house at night until black smoke curlicued around the edge of consciousness, and I awoke to the mercy of daylight, footsteps shuffling overhead.

In the rearview mirror of remembering, flamenco was the bridge between my departure from Detroit and my return, allowing me to visit lives where I didn't settle. Teaching Astrid how to dance the *sevillanas* let me try on her world: there were sleepovers and dinners with her family and weekend trips through the Andalusian countryside where the sun, white hot, devoured the grass, leaving a poverty of landscape. We'd skip school to wander Seville's Thursday flea market, taking selfies next to oversized pictures of the Pope. With its detritus of pre-internet life—musical instruments, mechanical toys, stamp collections, foreign coins, old photographs, roller skates, CDs, DVDs, crumbling paperbacks, and old electronics—the flea market existed in that liminal space between tradition and progress.

"I totally need this." Astrid was holding up a captain's wheel the size of a beach ball. "Ahoy, matey."

I snapped her picture.

"Don't post that yet. My mom called me in sick today."

"Lucky you. That means I'll be sitting in detention by myself tomorrow."

"Don't worry. I am sure I'll get in trouble for something else."

From some stall in the flea market came Adele's "Hello." Astrid sang like she was in church, guarding the captain's wheel to her chest, swimming her head above her shoulders for every refrain. Being with her felt like being in a movie.

"Who's your biggest heartbreak?" She asked when the song had ended.

It would be years before I realized it was my mother. I thought about Cody, our boarder back in Detroit, who was part of the reason I was in Seville, and my father with his smile like a billboard making a false promise, but I answered, "Daniel."

"Finally, a name is revealed."

"There's no name because it was over before it started." My eyes filled but didn't spill. "Someone Like You" played next. "Someone really likes Adele."

Astrid put the wheel down, her feet sliding into first position as she raised her arms above her head, fingers forming duck bills, and sang along with the verse while she danced the first *copla* of the *sevillanas*. As she turned, she grabbed my hand and pulled me into the dance. Changing places during the *pasada*, we sang the chorus in unison, and a few people gathered, some tossing coins between the spokes of the captain's wheel lying discarded on the ground. Egged on by the audience, Astrid sang louder, breaking the *sevillanas*, and took the song to me on one knee. I knelt, mirroring her posture, as we sang to each other about turning mistakes and regrets into bittersweet memories. Crooning the bridge, Astrid kicked her front leg back to turn herself as I scooched forward, so then we were kneeling side by side, arms draped over each other's shoulders, as we belted out the final refrain to each other. In the unreality of applause, our faces tipped forward, lips fitting, everything soft; she tasting of watermelon, our tongues wetter than waterslides. A few onlookers cheered as an embracing couple sharing a skateboard cruised by.

"Was that okay?" Astrid's fingers touched her lips as if to make sure they were still there.

"I—" I stopped my mouth. In the expandable quiet, I heard the petal soft chords of the *guajira*. "I've never kissed a girl before. Have you?"

"No." Her voice scaled. "Look." She pointed to the euros shining through the spokes of the captain's wheel on the ground and left me to gather them up. "We're rich."

"Should we celebrate?" My head jerked toward an old man dive bar bordering the flea market, its blue and white Moorish tiles visible through the huge windows which opened onto the street.

We sidled up to the counter, pinkies touching in its shadow, as Astrid ordered in German-accented English. The bartender hesitated before a "fuck it" moment passed over his face, and he went to pour us two beers.

We smothered our excitement; the getaway exuberance of criminals. "Shhh. Act cool. We are technically old enough to get served," she reassured herself, tossing her cockeyed hair, "no matter what our parents think."

"I've only ever been served at Daniel's family's place when he was working. I keep forgetting I'm allowed to drink here."

"Where is it?"

"On Plaza de la Alfalfa."

"What's it called?"

"Bodeguita Fabiola."

Astrid paid the bartender. "Let's get a table."

We each picked up a beer, and I followed her to a wooden high top, sticky with pint-glass rings. "I half expected him to reconsider and take these back."

"Way. I think it was my German accent that saved us. It's very commanding." She held up her glass. "*Salud.*"

"*Salud.*" I clinked her glass with my own. "To the *sevillanas.*"

"And Adele."

"And Adele."

We drank.

Astrid's bottom lip pulled down into a line. "That tastes like *scheisse.*"

"You get used to it. Wait. Is this your first beer?"

"As if." She gulped and coughed. "It tastes different in Germany." Astrid studied the contents of her glass. "Truth or dare."

"No."

"You have to."

"No."

"Come on." She clucked like a chicken.

"Aaaargh. Truth. No. Dare."

"I dare you to photograph that man's eyebrows." Astrid pointed to an old guy with caterpillars across his forehead. "From up close."

"No." I laughed into my hands. "Omigod, they've grown like an inch off his face. You could bead them."

"Stop staring." She whispered between giggles.

"You stop staring."

"Are you going to do it?"

I shook my head. "Truth."

Astrid leaned closer, her beer breath sticky on my cheek. "Okay. Have you had sex?"

I giggled harder.

"Omigod, you have! With Daniel?"

¡Tierra, traígame! My hand covered my eyes, and I nodded.

"Okay, so Daniel. Who else?"

I took my hand away. "No one. It was only him and only once." Later, when this story was scrawled in school bathroom stalls, it had morphed into multiple people and multiple times.

"Wow. He had sex with you and then ghosted. Humans can be garbage."

"It wasn't like that. It…" I thought about how the street lamps made lines of light on my belly, our bodies linking and then unlinking, the chaos between my legs. "I don't regret it."

"I want to see this guy."

"What about you?"

Astrid went to the bar and returned with two short glasses of brown liquid. "The finest of the house vermouth and the end of today's earnings."

"It looks like prune juice."

"Period blood."

I gave a moment of silence for decency. "Salud."

"*Salud.*"

"So, was he a blood cock or a sausage cock?"

I spit vermouth onto the table and gave Astrid a long look. "I think you've been waiting to spring 'cock' on me."

"Maybe. Blood or sausage?"

"I don't know what that means."

"A blood cock," Astrid looked at the table top for words, "starts out small but, umm, reaches its full potential." She assumed the air of a school lecturer. "A sausage cock, while well-sized at its restive state, never quite fills the tip." During this explanation, Astrid's accent had become uncannily British.

"Interesting." I giggled into my vermouth. "Blood cock." Under me, the floor began to slide. "Truth or dare?"

"Dare. I dare you to take me to Fabiola's so I can see this Daniel."

"No." I laughed harder.

"I can go without you."

"No! He may not even be working."

"From the look on your face, I think you hope he will be." Astrid was nodding her head like a puppy-dog car dash ornament. "You want to take me."

"I do?"

She was still nodding. "You do. You really do." She inclined her head toward mine, her lips leading.

I jerked my face back. "I'm sorry. I'm not…"

"What? I wasn't, so don't say that I was."

"I wouldn't."

"Okay." But she sounded like it wasn't.

"Okay."

"Drink up."

We drained our glasses.

A thousand little feet were kicking at my stomach as we cut through the city toward Fabiola's. When we got to Plaza de la Alfalfa, we staked a bench where we could watch the *bodeguita*. "I used to take Spanish classes there." I pointed to a white-washed building on the square. "It seems like a lifetime ago."

"How long has it been since you've seen him?"

I recalled the secret breathing of the river. "Not since that second dead girl turned up. "Omigod, there he is." My heart broadened. Daniel seemed taller, his hair longer, the first signs of spring's sun having kissed his skin.

"What's he doing?"

He had come out to clear a table. As he gathered an empty glass and napkin, something shiny snagged the afternoon light. "Looks like he's putting something in his pocket."

"Whoa." Astrid punched my arm. "You look like her." Astrid pointed at a woman leaving Fabiola's, paused in the doorway to don a pair of sunglasses, a shipwrecked look across her face. "You know, you never asked me who my biggest heartbreak was."

"My bad." I was half listening, watching Lola emerge from the darkness of Fabiola's doorway into a dazzle of sunlight, Daniel giving the tiniest of nods in her direction. "Who?"

"You."

# FANDANGOS

His name was Cody Ryan, and for years, I knew him. He lived in the bedroom adjacent to mine in Detroit. This was in our house on Longacre Way, a street checkered with empty lots, dilapidated buildings, and jungle-size weeds near Eight Mile Road, the dividing line between post-apocalyptic cityscapes and Detroit's pale suburbs. Cody made me Jell-O when I was home sick from school, taught me how to ice skate backwards, took me for Coney dogs at Duly's Place, where Albanian music blared from the kitchen, and the cooks danced around in their hair nets. If my mother was working overtime or making the four-hour drive to the Oaks Correctional Facility in Manistee, Cody would let me help him in his workshop—which was a part of our garage—a maniacal forest of metal frames, spare parts, and second-hand tools, a place where he would take broken or discarded things and make them like new. He specialized in chandeliers; huge fixtures of translucent, colored glass and brutalist metal accents which invoked the wild nature vining the ramshackle houses of our neighborhood. Glass icicles dripped from serpents of coiled wire; these were interspersed between metal branches, pussy-willowed with tear drop light bulbs, all mounted together inside hardware frames. His creations found homes in the high-end boutiques that sprang up in Eastern Market as the creative class gentrified Downtown and Midtown and left the rest of the city to decay. It was 2015, the year my father, a man I hadn't known for a long time, came back, and Cody left, and then I went away, and everything changed. Cody was thirty-three. He had been with my mother and me for almost half my life, after Fallujah, after he stopped having a regular job and started making things. I was sixteen: skeptical and resentful, a taut wire waiting to be tripped.

Most afternoons Cody tinkered in the garage, the smell of

nicotine between his fingers. He seldom spoke while he worked, preferring the sound of Tom Waits's smoke-scratched chords crackling into the gray-lit garage. Later in the day would come the smell of Irish Spring as Cody made sure to shower before Lila, my mother, came home. He'd pull a fresh T-shirt over his wiry frame before gelling back the Jesus curls that threatened his eyes. Sometimes, he'd shave. Those were the days he made deliveries. He'd bring his Frankensteined creations to women named Jessica or Ashley or Amber, women who smelled of Flowerbomb or Gucci Guilty, women who wore shearling motorcycle jackets over their off-the-shoulder tops and raw-hemmed denim, women who used chop sticks and spoke French, or so I imagined. He'd return late in the evening, long past retail hours, his hair hanging in his eyes, trailing a scent of abalone and amber. Then he'd see Lila. In a voice wisped with sunset, he'd ask my mother about her day, and his eyes would gloss with a look that made me look away. His final smell, the one that lingered in the folds of his clothes as he was driven from his bedroom to the living room sofa, was night sweat. I'd awaken in dawn's watery light, Detroit's storms shattering ice through trees or splattering rain against window panes, to find Cody on the couch, a blanket battled to the floor, his skinny legs bared to the damp chill. Listening to his whimpering, I'd cover him and wait before I gingered my way over the floorboards back to my bedroom. Cody never spoke about his nightmares. In the morning, I'd awaken to the smell of brewing coffee and find a plate of scrambled eggs or toaster-fresh waffles waiting for me. If my mother hadn't worked a late shift at the VA hospital (this was where she and Cody first met—she as a licensed, practicing nurse, he as a patient), she would join us. Although he was our boarder, they seemed like friends: speaking easily and laughing, laughing in a good way, not laughing at a joke or at a person, but laughing as if the whole world and being alive in it were fun.

After breakfast, I would go to school, the playground full of kids and balls, thrilled words, the wrong laughter. I'd find the other whitish kids who also had incarcerated fathers, kids who wore secondhand clothes and smelled of food-pantry bread. Some of us had known one another since elementary school, when a strobe of flashing red and blue light seemed like a spaceship landing on the front lawn and not a police car pulling up in front of your house to take your father away. We kids played tether ball together, joined and quit the Scouts together, smoked cigarettes at picnic tables in a Mexicantown park while we waited for someone's older brother or sister or cousin to buy us beer. I didn't smoke—once Cody let me take a drag off his cigarette, and I threw up—and seldom drank, my taste for beer not yet developed. I'd sit among the others, feeling conspicuous, and listen to snatches of Spanish being volleyed across the park. Sometimes, we'd play poker. The boys, tough with their Marlboro Reds and shot-gunned Bud Lights, would pull out Wonder Bread bags full of loose change. A deck of cards would appear, and one of them would shuffle. Few girls were allowed to play unless the game were strip poker. In our freshman year, when puberty was in full swing, some in the group would pair up, disappearing inside the folds of the park's leafy skirt and reappearing later with mussed hair and grass-stained jeans, the boy grinning at his friends, the girl looking at the ground.

One time, I was that girl.

I didn't spend much time at picnic tables after that.

Instead, I retreated to my bedroom, immersing myself in the enigma of Lorde and the wisdom of Adele. One Thursday in early March, I was on my bed, idly touching myself and won-dering when life would start when Cody knocked and entered my room. I thought he was going to ask me to turn my music down, but he just stood there.

"What?" I prompted.

Tension rode Cody's shoulders, his hands pocketed. "You don't have a chair in here."

He was still wearing the shirt he had slept in, which meant my mother was probably working late. "So?"

"Can I sit down?" He gestured to a corner of my bed.

This was someone I used to watch cartoons with lying toe to toe under a blanket on the living room floor. "Sure." I scooched over to make room, but Cody sat on the floor and stared at the hem of my blanket. There was a fresh blood blister on his index finger, and his knuckles were red. A car drove by, blaring "8 Mile" from its speakers. "What happened?" I gestured to his hand.

Cody shook his head. "I got mad at a piece of wood."

"Wood's such a dick," I said.

Cody laughed but only a little. "When did you grow up?"

"All at once. What's up? You almost never come in here."

"Not since *Where the Wild Things Are.*"

"Max and his onesie." I suddenly wanted him to read it to me again. "You're going to tell me something bad."

"It depends."

My stomach roller-coastered.

"Lila," his voice graveled. "Lila went to Manistee today."

Under a blanket, I curled and uncurled my toes. "So?"

"She went to Oaks. To pick up your father. He's getting out."

Cody's words were a jumble of puzzle pieces I couldn't quite fit together. His voice grew fainter as though the bedroom floor were widening, moving us farther apart. I had the urge to shout. "When will they get here?"

"Not until tomorrow." Cody cleared his throat. "Lila thought it might be easier to spend their first night at a hotel."

The small, dark part inside me grew hard. After everything my father had done, she still put him first. "If he's going to live with us, what's going to happen to you?"

Cody shifted. "I'm not sure."

"Everything's going to change."

He drew his knees up to his chest, a closed accordion.

We stilled, listening to the ringing silence. I waited for my bedroom to transform itself into a mysterious jungle, but it didn't. "Why didn't she tell me herself?"

"She didn't find out until after you'd left for school. I think she didn't want to interrupt your classes."

"She could have called after school and told me."

"I think the prison takes your phone when you enter."

"She could have called me from the road."

Cody rocked himself a little.

"When did she tell you?"

"This morning."

Outside my window, the trees were shadows in the fuzzed, cobalt light. I imagined Lila hanging up the phone, rushing to Cody in her excitement, hugging him wildly, he burying his face into her Medusa hair, letting her scent of coconut oil wash over him. It got hard to swallow. "Why did you wait so long to tell me?"

"I don't know." He rubbed at a stain on the floor.

"Forget it." I turned onto my side, facing the wall. I must have slept because when I shifted onto my back, the sky was bruised, and Cody had gone.

They pulled into the driveway early the next afternoon, the sun above vulgar with clarity. My mother was behind the wheel, sunglasses shading her eyes, while the man beside her sat back in his seat, looking out the windows. When he heard their car, Cody urged me from my bedroom and out the front door where we stood, an urban version of *American Gothic*.

My mother switched off the ignition. I imagined their interlaced fingers untangling across the front seat to a muttered count of three before both doors heaved open. From somewhere behind the house came the snap of dry branches breaking.

My father exited the car first, planting his feet on the ground and unfolding himself to his full height, which, while still tall, seemed less than I remembered. His face had aged: there were deep lines across his forehead and around his eyes, which were smart and mean, as if the time inside had threaded his veins with steel rods, pushing out the entirety of his blood. After all this time, seeing him was like diving into an ocean: first an intense cold shock, then just numb. Memories collided and spun: his

big hand oven-mitting my small one as I tripped over the hem
of my gypsy costume, trick or treating. A canary-yellow balloon
polka-dotted with white, laced around my tiny wrist, track marks
scoring his. There were Ferris wheel rides and Chuck E. Cheese
pizza parties and backyard barbecues, our skinny trees strung
with paper lanterns to rival the mating lightning bugs. Hushed
voices, whispers near the garage, dark laughter. Baggies. Days
with my father's towering frame snailed onto the living room
sofa, his violent shaking, vomiting. Sirens. Voices crackled with
police radio static before fists pounded the front door. Long
drives on empty highways through shadowy, pre-dawn light, the
plastic cold of the car's front seat biting the backs of my thighs,
rolls of quarters reeling forward and back between my mother
and me. Our car stopping outside a double chain-link fence.
Razor wire. Searches and inspections and birth certificates and
forms. Reaching on tiptoes to feed coins into vending machine
slots for photo cards and snack cakes and coca-colas. A quickly
filling visiting room. My mother, relaxing into her assigned seat,
wiping at the mascara smeared under her eyes.

My father would shuffle toward us in his prison issued
slippers, blue cotton pants, and blue cotton shirt with orange
across the shoulders. He was allowed to hug and kiss each of us
at the beginning and the end of the visit and when a picture was
being taken. They'd kiss until the photo cards ran out. His hugs
to my mother always lasted longer than his hugs to me, their
arms wrapping around each other as if they'd been enwombed
that way. Finally, we'd sit, they holding hands across the table,
lost in one another, as I pedaled the air with my feet, treading a
sea of invisibility. When Cody came to live with us, it was easier
for me not to go, until not going was the norm.

My father looked around, taking in the shaggy lawn next
door, overgrown with weeds, the house across the street with
its half sunken façade like a stroke victim's crippled face, rain-
grayed paper trash melded into the pavement, chunks of soiled
upholstery foam clogging up the gutters farther down the road.
At the end of our street sat a rampaged pair of easy chairs

covered in bird shit, gushing their guts onto the ground. I wondered how my father saw our street, the shape and contour the neighborhood had taken while he was on the inside, and what he had experienced in return. I stepped forward.

Lila walked around the back of the car to join my father, their arms garlanding each other's waists, his hand seeking out the lip of her jeans, his fingers snuggling into the crevice between skin and denim. She giggled, a sound like a glass bell, and whispered something in his ear. His laugh was a drum. Hot pins poked through my chest, and Cody's eyes searched the ground as if he had lost something. They moved toward us as a unit, sheening strange and bright.

I met them halfway, a tight fist in the back of my throat. Finally, I hugged my father, mostly because I thought I should, not because I wanted to. I side-hugged him, self-conscious about my boobs and curious about prison smell. It was there, a scent of desperation and decay, underneath the bottled herbal freshness of budget hotel shower gel. I pulled back as his eyes dampened. "You're all grown up, Lava." He turned to my mother. "I've missed so much." My mother kissed his shoulder and folded her other arm around me, drawing us together. The fist inside me loosened.

"It's okay." Lila kissed the side of his head as she broke her arm away from me. "We've got so much ahead of us." She still had one arm wrapped around my father. "Cody," she called. "What are you doing so far away? You're part of this family too."

Cody approached my father, his body straightening with military habit. "I'm Cody."

"Jesse."

They sized each other up.

My mother turned, putting her free arm around Cody's shoulder. "Let's get into the house. I'm starving."

I trailed behind them.

&

Money had always been tight, even when my father was a card

dealer at the Greektown Casino before his arrest. Now that he was a convicted felon, he couldn't get his gaming license reinstated, and no one wanted to hire him. He needed to pay criminal fines and court costs and restitution payments and parole fees. My mother's salary stretched thinner. She took on extra shifts, and Cody continued to live with us. We all sought ballast as the house shrank. There were waiting times for the bathroom as my father luxuriated in long, steaming hot showers or private, magazine-reading dumps. We often ran out of toilet paper, grateful as he was for its cotton-cuddle softness. There were the things you didn't miss until you couldn't have them. We couldn't keep any wine or beer or liquor in the house. A parole officer could show up at any time and search our home as he waited for my father to pee into a cup. (Once, an officer came when I was home alone. Instead of coming back later, he pushed his way into the house to make sure I wasn't hiding my father under my bed. He had me cornered between an armoire and the hallway wall, his slobbery lips coming closer, when Cody's truck pulled up. Cody wanted me to file a report, but Lila talked him out of it.) There were the things you never appreciated until you saw someone savor them. My father would play with switches—lights were his favorite—having been denied the right to turn something on or off when he wanted. He loved the living room throw rug. He'd walk back and forth, thrilled by the feel of synthetic fibers against his bare feet. He liked to investigate. He'd wander around the house, re-acquainting himself with every nook and cranny as he once did his eight by eight-foot cell. And there were the habits he could not break. He woke before 5 a.m., conditioned to do so for the 5 a.m. count. He ate really fast with his free arm curved around his plate as if he were protecting his food. He didn't make eye contact during meals, preferring to watch the sides of the room with his head down.

More revolutions of the clock. Jesse found a job with a company contracted by the city to clean public restrooms. He'd leave for work shortly after I got home from school and return after I had gone to bed. He'd been at his job for a few weeks when I found him waiting for me outside my bedroom door.

"Could you do your Pops a favor?"

I got a crawly-belly feeling. "Okay."

"I need you to pee in this." He handed me a small glass jar. From the garage came the blustered whirl of Cody's jig saw.

"You mean now? I don't have to go."

"Drink some water. I can wait."

Standing near the kitchen tap, I heard him call his work and tell them he'd be a little late. There was an emergency with his daughter. I wanted to kick the kitchen cabinets. Instead, I chugged a pint glass full of water with his eyes on my back.

"That's my girl," is what he said.

I stalked into the bathroom.

Outside the door was the pulse of footsteps.

"I can't go if you're listening."

There was the pad of retreating feet, and I was alone, listening to the buzz of the bathroom mirror light rival a fly trapped between the window and its screen. Unable to pee, I got up and rooted around the back of the cabinet underneath the sink, looking for something to read. I found a tattered copy of *Hustler* hidden behind a roll of paper towel and a plunger, its pages curled. The women inside were sad and obvious. Borrowing my mother's makeup, I painted my face before I took off all my clothes and pretzeled myself into shapes and angles in front of the bathroom mirror, trying on the models' expressions until they became my own. Then I sat on the cold tile floor with my mother's makeup mirror anchored between my thighs, studying my vagina. There was a knock on the door and an urge to hurry, which I ignored. Finally, I was ready. I sat on the toilet to fill the jar with a yellow lie and then washed my face clean. The jar was warm when I fastened its lid. Embarrassed, I wrapped it in toilet paper before handing it over to my father.

∽

A new kind of tension strained the house. There had been several recent police killings of unarmed Black and Brown men around the country. Coming home from school one day, I saw my mother, Cody, and Jesse through the kitchen window, arms flailing, hands gesturing, fingers pointing wildly, the kitchen table littered with coffee cups. I thought they were discussing Cody still living with us, but they were arguing about the *murderers* (Jesse's word) and the need for action. Jesse thought all police were corrupt, but Cody defended them. Jesse said that figured. Cody asked what that was supposed to mean, which was met with silence, and then Cody said the police officers he had fought with in Iraq were brave. Jesse said people ultimately stuck with their own kind and that was a lesson he, Cody, should learn. Then Jesse said he had to get to work.

"I thought you had tonight off. Did I misunderstand?" Lila brought their cups to the sink.

"I'm sorry baby. The boss is in a jam. I'll see if I can get home early." He put his hand over her throat and kissed her long and deep until Cody went into the garage, trailing the scent of old coins in a pocket. I followed.

"You haven't been out here for a while." Cody was sorting through prisms of red chandelier glass shaped like tears.

"I know." I picked a few pieces up and held them to the light.

"How are things?"

"You know. You live here." I pressed the glass against my neck. "What do you think?"

"It'll get better."

"Liar. And I meant about the chandelier drops. What do you think? Could you drill holes in these to make me a necklace?"

When Cody came forward to inspect the pieces, the air between us changed. I leaned into it. Time held still, then tilted as my mother entered the garage. Cody slid back, his eyes to her, out of reach. My face flooded with heat.

Cody coughed and then asked, "Do you want the holes drilled at the top or on the sides?"

"I—I don't care. Forget it."

"Why don't you find five more pieces of the same size and bring them to me?" He went over to his worktable and changed the bit on his Makita.

"What are you two doing?" Lila perched on a corner of his workbench.

"Making a necklace. Lava's got a good eye." Cody rummaged for a length of wire.

"I said forget it. I don't want one."

"I'll take one." Lila looked at Cody like a puppy looks at a ball.

The tops of Cody's ears turned red. "Okay. Do you want a pendant or a choker?"

When I left the garage, Cody was fitting a glass teardrop to the hollow at the base of Lila's neck.

The first glass jar begot another and another and another.

"I don't want to do this anymore." I made a beeline for my bedroom, but Jesse blocked my way.

"What's wrong?" His eyes had a souped-up shine.

"I feel…It's weird."

"Look, I know, but…but I'm doing this for your mother." Then, "And you."

"I don't believe you. Why do you need it?"

His eyes scanned the living room and stopped on an old photograph of my mother with her cousin Lola in Spain. In the picture were two young women, variations of the same paper doll, dancing on a rooftop. A smudge of an old man sat playing the guitar underneath a clothesline. Both girls were wearing dresses cascading with wedding-cake exuberance, their hair swept high on their heads, anchored by a single flower. Their left arms extended toward each other, curved fingers almost touching, while their right arms formed crescent moons above their heads. Their teenage faces were smiling, their secret future dreams indefatigable. Jesse went over to the photo and brought it close to his face. "I sell it."

Lunch revisited my mouth. I swallowed it down. "To who?"

"Whoever needs it."

"Why?"

"We need the money. Supervised probation costs eighty bucks a month plus drug-testing fees. I still owe for the lawyer and court." He caressed the image of my mother beneath the glass and then put the picture down. He turned to face me. "I want Lila to stop working so many extra shifts."

A new fear feathered me. "Does she know?"

"Of course not. And you can't tell her. I want her life to be easier."

I took the jar, willing a sense of erasure.

"You don't have to." Cody's entrance from the garage uncorked my fatigue. The floor beneath my feet sagged.

"It's none of your business." Jesse stepped in front of me.

Cody ignored him. "Lava?"

Something slippery swelled in my mind.

"I said, this is none of your business. She's not yours. Either of them."

Cody got snagged on a barb of accusation. "What's that supposed to mean?"

"You don't think I see the way you look at my wife? The way your eyes follow her around."

"You've got it wrong."

"I don't think so bro. Why are you still living here?"

"Because Lila needs me."

"She needs *me*. This is my family, not yours. She feels sorry for you."

"Dad—"

"She's afraid you're going to crack up again. That's why she lets you stay."

Cody was unhinging. "I help her. With money. With Lava."

"You'd love to 'help' Lava. You're the one who should be locked up."

Fists connected to faces. There were gut punches, kicks, the sound of bone cracking. Something glinted off the overhead light. A hot slice of pain. I didn't realize I was screaming until I saw my father's knife stuck in my arm.

Lila ran inside the house, a bag of groceries cradled in her arm, her car keys in hand. My father collapsed onto the living room rug, vomiting. Cody, with an eye swelling, was supporting my arm to keep the knife steady.

"What happened?" Lila's grocery bag fell to the floor as she went to Jesse.

"Lila, we need to call 911." Cody dug into his back pocket.

"No." My mother stuck two fingers in my father's mouth to scoop out the vomit before grabbing a pillow to elevate his head. "I know the drill." She checked his vitals.

"Not for him. For Lava."

This time my mother looked at me, the knife in my arm registered. "Lava, are you dizzy?"

"No." Still, my mother didn't come. She ran into her bedroom and returned with her first aid kit, some socks, and a blanket, which she wrapped around Jesse, who had started shivering,

"Cody, put your phone down. Can't you see he's been using? He'll get sent back."

Cody held his phone but didn't dial.

"If you care about me, us, at all." Lila's plea was a drawbridge to tears.

The phone slid back into Cody's pocket.

"I can't believe you." I shrieked. "He did this to himself."

"Lava, calm down." Finally, she came to me. "You need to keep your arm still." She wrapped the bandages around the socks to form a donut, which she slipped over the knife to steady it. "Cody, you can let go now. Thanks. Go get some ice for your eye, and then I need you to stay with Jesse to make sure he doesn't choke if he vomits again while Lava and I go into the kitchen." Lila waited for Cody to leave. "He's your father, and he's sick, and we need to help him." Her voice hushed, mantling a momentary calm. "Just like I am going to help you. Understand?"

Cody returned with a bag of frozen peas over his eye.

"We're all we've got." Lila gave Cody a grateful smile. "Cody, watch Jesse please. Lava, we're going into the kitchen, where

I'm going to take the knife out. It may hurt. There might be some blood, depending on how deep the cut is, but it's going to be fine. Then I am going to disinfect it, which will hurt, and then I'll sew you up, which will also hurt. I need you to be brave. Are you ready?"

The next days were tense and shadowed, the house and garage empty after Cody's departure. My mother stayed at home, rubbing Jesse's back or legs and giving him alcohol sponge baths in between his bouts of diarrhea and vomiting. When she knocked on my bedroom door carrying a glass jar, I knew what to do.

It was more or less the same crew haunting the picnic tables. The bread bags full of coins were gone, but there was still beer and now, joints, to be shared, beginner sips of whiskey. I sat down and inhaled, long and deep, relishing the harsh pull of oxygen from my lungs. Numbed, I listened to the twilight bugs beguiling one another, cooing and camouflaging before they spread their wings and took flight.

# ESCOBILLA

*Escobilla:* An extended flamenco dance sequence of intricate footwork combinations.

*Escobilla:* (feminine noun) A brush. A tool for cleaning. I flipped the light switch, its swinging bulb shadow dancing with the wall. In the silent scream of the rehearsal room, memories flitted here and there until I caught up, the past and the future's past merging. *I didn't think it'd be your first time.* There was snow in Detroit but rain in Seville. Ice rippled like someone had screamed into Lake St. Clair, and it froze that way. Orange trees wept on a Mudéjar palace, the royal gardens fragrant with wet leaves and citrus. *Truth. Dare.* I clapped the heartbeat of a *siguiriya*, letting it echo in the cocoon of the room. *Juega para mi Papá.* The toe of my shoe rebounded against the floor—*okay*—but didn't exorcise the haunting in my head.

*I didn't think it'd be your first time. Truth. Dare. Juega para mi, Papá. Okay. I didn't think it'd be your first time.*

Yellow thoughts reverberated, took shape, and chimed.

*Truth. Dare. Okay. Didn't think. Papá.*

*Think.*

*Dare.*

*Okay.*

*Papá.*

*Truth.*

I thumbed over the word while the tip of my shoe scraped back and forth, holding the asymmetrical rhythm. Telling the truth had fueled a lie and doubled its throw. People got carried away. Stories trailed me through the school hallways, louder than roller skates on Detroit gravel, flowering through Facebook threads, trellis feed. I struck my heel against the floor to purge the swirl of words. One strike became many until I was dancing on language. Outside the studio window, the sun hinted beneath the clouds.

*DARE. DARE. DARE. DARE. DARE.*

I beat both heels against the floor, the *golpe* mutating into a *tacón* step, the increased tempo transforming my heels into machine-gunfire, me a sadistic child. The studio door opened and shut, a phantom guest, as I passed my hands over my eyes to wipe a duck row of faces from an imaginary target line. Spent by speed, my stamping heels dawdled, the beat morphing into giving up. Time slowed; I held it in the palm of my hand, my diaphragm, a butterfly's wings. In. Out. Like a needle sewing flesh. In. Out. Like heart ventricles, beating. In. Out. Like a cell door closing. In… Outside the pane was the watery afterbirth of rain.

*Okay?????*

My left foot slid forward as my right struck the floor. Practicing the *chaflán*, I was both absent and present, sliding back to a girl's kiss, back to a boy's lips, the pewter river, his dick, a glass bottle, my piss. Strike. My foot, this floor. *Okay.* A four-letter word that sounded like two. *OK?* Slide. *Okay.* Strike. Both question and answer. Sliding, slipping back, keys slid under a crumpled napkin. A pillow slid under a puking head. A bottle slipped into my cupped hand. My foot slid forward, absenting me in the present; presenting me in the past, Lola donning sunglasses, a shipwrecked look. Lila, strobed in red/blue light, a shipwrecked look. My striking foot slowed to the sound of a marble rolling down steps.

*I didn't think it'd be your first time.*

*I. Didn't. Think.*

*Didn't think. Didn't think. Didn't.*

*Think.*

The undoable do-over. The tip of my toe struck the floor behind my standing leg, rebounded to ankle height, and then struck the floor again and again and again, jackhammering. My first time, but not his, I was on my back, and he was on my front, jackhammering. Not his first time, not Lola's. How many times? Jackhammering. I repeated the *punta* with the opposite leg, the tip of the toe pounding the floor. Pow-pow-pow-pow-pow-pow. My eyes focused on a nameless elsewhere. Pa-pa-pa-pa-pa-pa-pa.

*Papá.*

I marked time with my heel until the *taconeo* surrendered. In the stillness of the room, my weight shifted from side to side. Pa. Pa. I stretched upward and then collapsed like a rag doll, flamenco's *sentimientos fuertes* rushing out along the hill of my back and onto the floor. A finger walk of vertebrae brought me to standing as a fleece of clouds unwrapped the sun. My arms lifted skyward, hips rocking. Pa. Pa. My arms twirled air, and memories spun: me sitting upon shoulders, as high as tree tops, trying to touch the clouds, in a vellum of pot smoke. A tricycle with pink cellophane tassels hanging from the handlebars, the weight of a hand letting go of the bike seat, the echo of footsteps trailing behind. There were snowballs and snow angels and crack pipes and pee bottles, pa, pa. My arms windmilled, elegant in their violence, matching the growing furor in my feet, turning me into a griffin. Sweat beaded my hair, raining onto the floor, cleansing me.

# SIGUIRIYAS

Her name was Lila Guajardo, and for years I knew her as my mother. This was on Longacre Way, in Detroit, Michigan, where we lived until my father Jesse went away. Lila and Jesse threw outdoor barbecues in summer, carved jack-o'-lanterns for Halloween, salsa danced in the living room when Detroit's winter hushed the streets, cloaking all the houses in snow. If my father was working late at the casino, Lila would set me up at the kitchen table with a large pad of white paper and a bundle of colored markers while classical guitar music played in the background. I would draw, and she would study from the thick books she used in her nursing-school night classes. Sometimes, after she put me to bed, I'd lie awake, listening to the soft panther of footsteps as she danced what I came to know as flamenco. Having snuck out of bed and hidden myself behind the threadbare edges of Jesse's chair, I'd watch as passion and pride currented through her body, curlicuing her spine into a sea creature's before mercurial footwork wiled Lila from one direction to the next. If she discovered me, the danced enchantment broke, and I was ushered back to my bedroom, the memory of flamenco staining the floor. Other times, flamenco coursed through Lila like a spate of rage, her quick-fire shuffles and sharp, cutting stamps spurning the music as it absorbed the collateral nature of her intuition. These were the times when Jesse came home as I was getting on the school bus, his eyes Bing cherries, his face sweaty. Lila would block the doorway, her bony arms woven across her chest, while Jesse stared at her until something primal charged the force field between them. Lila's mutinous arms would unknot, giving Jesse permission to take one of her hands, which he pressed to his heart as he crossed the threshold, and they lost themselves in the dark quiet of the house as my hand pressed to a school bus window, mid-wave.

When the school bus returned me, Jesse would be eating an early dinner as Lila kept him company at the kitchen table, the two held aloft in the scaffolding of their own private language. These were the before days; the days of a fully stocked bar, the days of a packed pantry and filled refrigerator. The days before Jesse was handcuffed, the days before Lila became hag-ridden. Before fear was thrown into my limbs and ran in me like a river. Before I mainlined the vocabulary of flamenco, before flamenco arranged what had been left unfinished. Two thousand fifteen marked the end of before. In 2015, Lila boxed up her hopes and dreams and packed two suitcases. I was sixteen—my insides honeycombed, dripping with underage rage—and on my way to Seville.

Although Lila had been born near the shallow streams and sand dunes of the Guadalquivir River delta, she grew up among the tortilla factories of La Bagley, near the Detroit River. Her parents had emigrated from Spain during the post-Franco economic devastation of the early 1980s, but every summer, unsettled longing drove the family back to Andalusia, where Lila and her cousin Lola, holding youth in their bodies, pursued flamenco. To dance flamenco was to uncork yearning; to dance it well was to glimpse an angel's wing. They'd batter rehearsal room floors as they learned how their bodies worked and later, how their bodies loved. Lila's limbs moved like wind chimes in a storm whereas Lola could launch her body like a rainbow, outsmarting gravity. After classes, they'd take to the summered streets where flamenco was truly learned. Fueled by the *sentimentos fuertes* of adolescence, their movements were words generating heat, reinventing space as they gave themselves to the *palos*. Passersby would gather, beguiled by the dancing teens cusped on womanhood, their long black hair swinging out like skirts, their lives nearly touching. Guitarists, strumming a gut sharing of happiness and suffering, vied to play for them, for flamenco was built on life's longing and heartbreak, and Lila and Lola were ripe to be loved. In the forgotten hours of before-morning, they'd bed down in abandoned buildings and play at being what they might become before scurrying to the family home to play at being what was expected of them. Or so I imagined.

Lila rarely spoke of her youth; the late-night flamenco dancing was her sole, expressed trespass of memory. In our Detroit living room, there was a photograph of two look-alike young women in long ruffled gowns dancing on a rooftop, the cupola of a nearby church casting a shadow behind them. The ribbon of my imagination spun from there, bundling the contents of an old shoebox I found tucked in a corner of Lila's closet, into the folklore of my ancestry. I'd flip through loose pictures: a photo of a jeans-clad woman slapping her upper thighs while her feet stamped an unheard rhythm, a dark sheet of hair wrapping her face, the slightest hint of a baby bump signaling the growing life inside her. An older woman wearing dark trousers with a skid of glittering polka dots down the side seams, throwing her head back with her mouth wide open, an arthritic hand clawed in front of her heart, pulling a song from the air. A creased photocopy of a sonogram. A rolled and rubber-banded flamenco poster depicting a dancer's back, the white tiered ruffles of her dress arching up like a squirrel's tail above her head. A pair of cloth, bougainvillea earrings faintly fragrant with orange blossom. An oversized hair comb studded with yellowing rhinestones, a few strands of long black hair enmeshed in its teeth. Handwritten letters in Spanish on pages torn from composition notebooks in the curvy cursive of adolescence, the pages' spiral bound edges missing a few confetti teeth. Official-looking documents, also in Spanish, which I could not decipher.

The first time Jesse went away was Vaselined in a memory of flashing lights, scored by Lila's begging beneath tears. In his absence, Lila body-battered loneliness. She stopped eating, her edges seeming to grow fainter and more translucent as her face became a photograph; her eyes big black shadows, her skin bleached to paper white. There were moments of pulse when Lila went to work or bought groceries or made me dinner, but for the most part, she was miles from mother. At night, she'd dance as if she could wrap pain in a thick skin of movement, no longer caring if I saw. She'd walk a sober, rough and faltering meter back and forth over the same spot on the kitchen floor, her steps making blunt, loud, sharp impacts. The driving pulse of her heels to the floor sounded like impatience, finger snaps marking time. Instead of the graceful, curved arm movements she usually employed, her arms were matchsticks, forming straight lines in front of her heart or cutting geometric shapes across her torso. Her treacherous feet would climax in a series of double-quick steps as though the woman Lila used to be was sending out an SOS from the cavernous place life without Jesse had hidden her. The small smacks of her steps stretched into infinity until what was twined with what would be, for flamenco was music that had no end. Dancing to the edge of self, her body yelled a corporeal prayer as flamenco's canon percussed through her. Lila suspended between this world and the next, amniotic, until she broke and never danced flamenco again.

Memories recollected. Buffer fence. Double chain link fence. Razor wire. Electronic detection system. Guard patrols and dogs and gun towers. Eleven buildings. 262,673 square feet of floor space. Four times one-hundred ninety-two men. Eyes watching. Lemon-scented, all-purpose cleaner. Commissary ramen. Eyes watching. The shush-shush of prison-issued slippers along vinyl-sheet floors. The startle of a cell block buzzer. Sleepy, beefy skin-stank. Eyes watching. Jesse and Lila, embracing, forming a flesh circle, oblivious to everything but each other; a dance at ease. Eyes watching. A leftover feeling. Another buzzer—visiting hours over. Jesse ushered out, Lila moving, her legs like water rushing reeds. Back inside the car, a spine stiffened. The silent ride back to Detroit, Lila steeled.

With Cody's arrival, Lila's spine uncluttered; her hips swam loose. The pain covering her face was carried away on the small backs of baby steps: Cody and Lila would cross paths in the kitchen, Lila having just come from work and still wearing her coat, Cody's dirty hands dragging the smell of sawdust and copper pennies, and they'd strike up a conversation that last-ed longer than the episode of *Veronica Mars* I'd be watching. They started making dinner together, sometimes sharing beer from the same glass. They played card games while I did my homework, almost-parents, volleying looks over hand-fans of hearts and spades, diamonds and clubs before Lila watched me brush my teeth, and Cody read to me in bed, his hair as black as a record album. If I had a sleepover, they might shoot pool at Temple Bar or go bowling. Lila would pick me up the next morning, her face melancholy, flamenco music mourning from her iPhone.

Lila's face gathered light as she prepared to visit Jesse in pris-on while the Oaks Correctional Facility frightened me with its bad smells and men with arms like maps. I'd beg to stay home, my voice, a clap of thunder from behind my locked bedroom door, until a threat or bribe moved me. The lunar landscape of Cody's face became eclipsed as we packed ourselves into Lila's car before daybreak. Leaving Cody alone felt like abandoning him at the bottom of a lonely well, and only our return could rescue him. We'd pull into the driveway and find the rain gutters swept clean of dead leaves or the picture window devoid of rain streaks and wind dirt. Household projects absorbed Cody's PTSD energy, but it was his acts of kindness that brokered Lila's trust, and I used this to my advantage. I'd feign sickness when she was running late for work, so she'd have no choice but to leave me in his care. I'd miss the bus, so he'd offer to pick me up from school when she was working the late shift. I'd forget permission slips or report cards that needed signing, so he'd autograph them last minute to maintain Lila's charade of a functioning family. It was a natural next step to leave me in his care for a Saturday or Sunday if I did not want to make the four-hour drive to Oaks. Instead of chaos, Cody provided calm. In the simplicity of his workshop, he taught me how to saw and sand and drill, to see possibility in the broken and abandoned. And when my father came back, he fought for me to have a chance at myself and not become a Lila.

I fought with Lila because I could. Staring at a face much like my own, I sought my edges inside the cold of argument. She didn't flinch. As the hours stretched long, as they do after arguing, I'd flee the house, wandering the bankrupt, unlit streets, making promises to myself, kicking rocks, stones turning over years. I'd enter abandoned, graffitied buildings reeking of cat piss and shit, and dance on the space between reason and emotion, obliterating it. Ignorant of form, I danced through the past, the space between movements carrying the history of them. When Cody left, I danced on thought, obliterating consciousness, ignoring the rules that kept a family civilized.

There were slow, measured footsteps in the hallway before Lila knocked on my bedroom door one Wednesday evening in May. I hoped she'd come to check on me, to see how I was taking Cody's hasty departure, or if I wanted to talk about Jesse's obvious addiction, or if my arm hurt and how it was healing. I was on my bed, turned to the wall, calculating the probability of my passing tenth grade and the degree to which I cared, when I heard the door open and then felt my mattress shift as she sat down. I turned my head and looked at her dirty hair, her collapsing mouth. There was a stain of vomit on her T-shirt, skid marks from Jesse's ripe, wild ride through withdrawal. Lila gazed through my bedroom window at the abandoned house on the other side of our yard, listening to the scrape of a tree branch against the side of the house.

"Have you heard from Cody?" I asked. Whenever I tried calling him, he didn't answer.

"I need to ask you something."

My skin bristled. I turned onto my back and peered at her from under my eyelids. In her hand was a small, glass jar. "How long have you known?" I asked.

"He told me today. I thought he might have been buying it."

"He told me he was *selling* it."

"Probably that too."

"I don't get it."

She shifted her weight as if she might reach out to me but

didn't. "He used your urine to pass his drug tests. When there were leftovers, he probably sold it. I know it's a lot to take in." Her eyes pocketed. "He did it for us."

My ribcage spread like wings. "He told me he did it for you, so you wouldn't have to work so hard."

Lila rolled the jar between her hands. "I'm still working hard."

Ants crawled on the underside of my skin as my breath stalled, and hope uncoiled.

"It's just until he's clean again." She held out the jar.

The bed seemed to expand, bringing me to the edge. I rolled back toward the wall in a log of silence. A slow rage heated my ribcage.

When she spoke next, her voice had honeyed, "Your arm's healing well."

"It still hurts a little."

She stroked my hair, which I felt in the base of my spine. My mouth opened a little.

"I'm not going to sell it," she whispered in my ear.

My emotions doubled back, betraying the undefended parts of me. Lila kept her hand on my shaking shoulders until they quieted. The mattress shifted again before the door closed. The glass jar, full of nothing, was waiting on my bedside table.

I first met Lila when she was born with the pulse of flamenco running through her. From my hiding place, her unguarded body spoke to me through stamps and turns as Lila danced the story of her life, for within flamenco beat the beauty and the underbelly of living. Watching, I'd be swept up by the glide of her arms or hypnotized by the fury in her feet, not realizing I was holding my breath until the tiny-girl cage of my chest felt like it might burst. On chubby legs, I'd race back to my room and gulp air, readying myself to practice what I had just seen.

I first met Lila in her childhood, in the Andalusian summer respites that interrupted the crime and violence of her school days in Detroit. Fueled by flamenco, longing scissoring through them, Lila and her cousin cusped womanhood in rehearsal rooms grown pheromonic with sweat. Their bodies ripened under the gaze of guitarists whose eyes had gone dark and buttony with pleasure. Flamenco liberated the nesting doll at Lila's core, freeing her to live outside the lines of life in an enclave of passion and pathos.

I first met Lila through a film of pot smoke while I was sitting upon Jesse's shoulders, and Lila was holding one of his hands. I wanted to touch the cotton-ball clouds, my dimpled arms reaching up, stretching higher, losing balance, falling backward, Jesse too high to catch me, Lila's body breaking my fall.

I first met Lila when she picked pieces of glass from the bottom of my bare foot with tweezers. I had stepped on a crack pipe in our backyard while catching fireflies in a mason jar.

I first met Lila in the strobing light of a police car as her face tin-manned with tears, Jesse, handcuffed and wobbling between the officers on either side of him. Lila rushed them, begging for one more moment, before a billy club blocked her, and a voice asked if she wanted to be arrested too for assaulting a police officer. *Think of your little girl, ma'am, and step the fuck back.* Jesse was charged with possession with the intent to distribute, done in by baggies full of snowflakes and shiny, blue-white rocks.

I first met Lila when she stopped talking and eating and washing because Jesse was sentenced to ten to fifteen years and a twenty-five thousand dollar fine. First the refrigerator emptied and then the cupboards. Bills collected on the kitchen table, unpaid. I missed the start of the school year. There were visits from truant officers and social workers, but few friends. When Jesse was finally awarded visiting privileges, life breathed back into Lila.

I first met Lila when she brought a boarder named Cody home to live with us, and I heard her laugh for the first time since I could remember. I watched their easy way together, how they gave each other ballast, and how, for a short while, he soothed her ache of loneliness when the panther of flamenco rustled Lila with primal need.

I first met Lila when she switched off from Cody, buffering the distance between them with me. She volunteered for night shifts, so she could bank hours and visit Jesse more often, suddenly agreeable to my staying back in Detroit with Cody. She volunteered for extra shifts, so she could keep Jesse's prison account flush with cash for phone calls, video calls, emails, and the commissary. In her absence, I absorbed Cody's attention, which kept me from being motherlessly depressed, until the onslaught of adolescence molded my face into Lila's. I was invited less and less into Cody's tobacco musk workspace and relegated to the script of school girl while he went out on deliveries.

I first met Lila through the polite gloss of her indifference, which made me wonder whose idea it was to have a child.

I first met Lila when she told Cody he'd have to leave for the good of the family. Arms dangling at his sides, his hands two useless trowels, Cody's face shut off. He packed his clothes. He packed his tools. He packed his truck. I watched from the translucent shield of my bedroom window as his all-weather tires churned gravel, and he left without a word of protest, which sounded like the opposite of family.

I first met Lila through the clear glass of an empty jar. The moment she left it on my nightstand was the moment we stopped being the people we had always been in the place where we were. Childhood left my body as I walked down the hallway of family, out the front door and into a Mexicantown park where everyone was drinking and smoking pot at a picnic table. I sat down among the Bud Light breath and Jack Daniels skin, angry, neat. Fury beat thought from my skull making me more everyone than anyone; I toked up, I threw down until my face was feathers. To return home, I navigated my rage with a swag and strut, the language of flamenco already inside me.

I first met Lila inside the architecture of my retribution. After a dehydrating morning when I held my pee until I thought I would burst, I frothed into an empty glass jar, miles away from daughter. I handed it back to Lila, and then she emptied it into a plastic baggie which she sandwiched between hand warmers.

Second thoughts reverberated in my head like footsteps on stairs, the sound of leaving.

Loving someone can defeat you.

∾

I walked home from school, lagging behind the trash blowing in the wind. When I reached the house, the living room curtains were still drawn. In my ears, the sharp staccato of heel stamps raced my heartbeat as I stood outside the front door, heeding instinct. There was no river of forgetting to cross. Lila was waiting for me on the sofa, still wearing her jacket, but Jesse was nowhere in sight. Inside me, some inner electricity switched on.

"How could you?" Her destroyed face.

The oven clock ticked hard.

"Just tell me why." Her expression shifted as her internal motor revved, and I gaped at her pain. She stood, tension riding the hanger of her shoulders. "Why ruin him?" She stalked up to me, her rebellious hair catching the light.

Eye to eye, I dug through my roots, looking for traces of us. "Ruin him? He was the one ruining us."

She grabbed my wounded arm. "Tell me why."

"You're hurting me."

"I don't care." She pressed and twisted my bandage.

"He's a piece-of-shit addict. We're better—"

She slapped my face, painting it red. For a moment I was stunned, then fascinated, and finally triumphant. When I slapped her back, I understood how my branches grew. Love is not the force of human progress.

"You need to leave." Her eyes flattened like a threatened animal.

"Fine." I spun on my heels and marched toward the stairs to my bedroom.

"This house."

I veered my direction. "Fine."

"For good."

My feet sputtered and stopped. "Where am I supposed to go?"

"I don't care."

"Some mother you are."

"Says the daughter who sabotaged her father's urine."

"You can't throw me out. This is my house too."

"Not anymore. I pay the mortgage. I buy the food. I decide who lives here, and I can barely look at you. So. You. Will. Go."

"Mom, please—"

"Don't you DARE—" She shook her head to hold her tongue. "Pack a bag and go." She reached inside her coat pocket and took out her wallet. "Give me your house keys."

'What?"

She held out a bunch of twenties. "Keys."

"What about school?"

"What about it? Go if you want."

"What about—"

"You should have thought about 'what about' before you skunked your pee."

"I'm, I'm sorry." Tears ran down my cheeks.

"It's a little late for that." Her voice cracked but held. "He's been re-arrested and will probably be sent back to Oaks." She looked at the money in her hand and put a few bills back into her wallet. "Go pack a bag and leave, or leave now. Either way, I can't have you here."

I took in her skin and hair, so like my own. In that moment, we were human together, but there was no alternative story to pin us down. She held out her empty hand. When I gave her my house keys, she gave me the dollars, and I shoved them into my pocket before she changed her mind.

Up in my bedroom, I turned to look for someone, turned to look for someone, turned to look for someone. Leaning against my bedroom door, I had no idea how to start. I remembered Lila's old shoebox filled with keepsakes and realized there was nothing here to be saved. My *Divergent* and Pharrell Williams posters could stay on the walls forever. I grabbed some underwear, socks, T-shirts, and jeans and stuffed them with my phone charger into a backpack as my eyes puddled in my face.

I went into the bathroom and grabbed my toothbrush and all the toiletries Lila and I shared, figuring she owed me because I had made her better off without him. Coming out, I heard the low rumble of Lila talking in Spanish on the phone. I dumped everything I was holding onto my bed and sat for a moment, listening to the rush of traffic outside the window, as a cradle of twitching wires crackled throughout my chest.

I finished packing and went downstairs, hoping that Lila might have changed her mind, but she was gone. The floor played tug of war with the ceiling. I wandered first through the kitchen, where my childhood heights charted a wall, and then into the living room, my eye landing on the picture of Lila, dancing flamenco with her cousin on a rooftop, before she tamped down her wild parts. Jesse loved that photo too. I grabbed it and stuffed it into my backpack as Cody's truck pulled into the driveway. I ran outside as his window unrolled.

"What are you doing here?"

"Lila called me."

"So did I. A lot. Why didn't you ever call me back?"

"I couldn't."

"Why not?"

"I just couldn't."

"That's bullshit." I didn't feel like torturing meaning out of his words. "Anyway, are you coming in, because if you are, she isn't here."

"I know. I am supposed to text her after I pick you up, so she knows it's safe to come back."

"Safe?" It stung like the bite of an invisible insect. "Is that because I slapped her? Because she slapped me first. And look what she did to my arm." The top of my bandage had darkened with blood seeping through from the underside.

"She asked if you could stay with me for a little while."

"How long?"

"She didn't say."

"Don't I get a say?"

"I don't think so. Do you have all your stuff?"

"I have my backpack." My stomach pretzeled. "Do I need more?"

Cody killed the engine. "I don't know." He turned, and his eyes slow-circled my face. "I understand why you did it."

"She told you?"

"She called me after he pissed hot."

"What did she say? Besides the obvious. I mean, does she hate me? Did you tell her I—I don't know, that…did you defend me?"

Cody hesitated before answering. "No."

"No? You just said you understood why I did it. Why didn't you say anything?"

Cody rubbed at an invisible stain on the steering wheel.

"I can't believe you didn't stick up for me."

"Would it have made a difference?"

I leaned against the truck door, looking at the house as my present shrank, and the future ran away. "Do you think I shouldn't have done it?"

"What I think doesn't matter. You're the one who needs to be good with what you did."

My mind flashed to all Cody's restless nights, battling his demons on the living room sofa.

"Go get your backpack, and then let's get some Coney Dogs. I'm starving."

"What do you do with it?" I wiped under my eyes before turning back to him.

"With what?"

"The love you have for her. The love she doesn't return. Where do you put it?"

It was Cody's turn to look at the house.

"On a remote island where the other wild things are." Cody laughed a single "ha."

"Have you always loved her?"

"Almost." Cody shook his head a little. "You were there. How much do you remember?"

"Enough. I wish she had picked you."

Cody rapped his knuckles against the dashboard. "I don't think we get to pick."

"Do you know why she doesn't love me?"

Cody handed me a tissue. "She does Lava. She's just forgotten right now."

"How long till she comes out of amnesia?"

He looked at me with his tired, hanging eyes.

The silence was accusatory. I scurried to get my backpack like a careful rat.

⤚

Life at Cody's felt like a rehearsal. As long as I went to school, I could come and go as I pleased, so I was surprised when he picked me up from class one day the following week. Instead of driving to his apartment, he headed toward Lila's.

"What are you doing? Does she know we're coming?" I didn't think Cody had an ambush in him.

"She called and asked me to bring you over. She wants to talk to you."

"About what?"

"She didn't say."

"I don't believe you. What did she say?"

Cody kept his eyes on the road.

"How did she sound?"

"Tired."

"Did she seem like she was ready to forgive me?"

"I don't know." But he looked like he did. We rode in silence.

As we turned onto Longacre Way, Cody reached over and squeezed my hand. "No matter what happens, you're going to be okay."

I was looking at him when the "For Sale" sign stuck in our lawn snagged the corner of my eye. "Oh my God! She's moving? That's what she wants to talk to me about? Is she taking me with her?"

"Let her explain."

"Oh my God, you do know."

Cody pulled into the driveway. "She's waiting for you inside."

"Aren't you coming?"

"She asked me to stay in the car."

I stood in front of the doorbell, wishing I could outsmart gravity. Lila opened the door and stood there for a while. The silence was a test. Stepping aside to let me in, she told me to go into the kitchen, where we sat down on opposite sides of the table. She seemed like an actor hired to play a version of herself in a made-for-TV melodrama. It had been only ten days since I had seen her, but those ten days eclipsed our years together.

"You're selling the house?"

"Yes." She kept her eyes focused to the right of my ear.

"Why?"

"Your father is." She stopped to clear her throat. "Is back at Oaks, and, and it will be easier to visit him if I am closer."

I registered the "I," not a "we," and nodded my head. "Where are you moving?"

"I'd rather not say."

A mousetrap pain. I blinked hard "Can I get some water?"

Lila nodded.

At the sink, I let the water run longer than it needed before I opened a cabinet door to get a glass. Most of the cups and dishes were gone. I grabbed hold of the sink, looking into the open cabinet for someone to reflect my shock back to me. "When are you leaving?"

"I'm not sure yet."

"Where am I going?"

"That's why I wanted to talk to you. Why don't you sit back down?" I crossed back to the table as she pulled out an envelope from under the napkin holder and slid it toward me. "I talked to my cousin Lola in Spain, and we thought it'd be a good idea if you went to live with her for a while."

My feet felt like they were slipping off the floor. "For how long?"

"It depends."

"Don't I need a passport?"

"It's in the envelope with your ticket."

"What about my stuff?"

"I've packed you two suitcases. They're in the garage."

"What if I don't want to go?"

"You don't really have a choice. You can't stay at Cody's forever." She picked up her phone, and a moment later, I heard the motorized clatter of the garage door opening.

"I could come with you."

"That is not an option."

"But Mom—"

She winced as if bee-stung. "Don't," she said before she cleared her throat. "I spoke to your school, and since you need to repeat the year anyway, they're allowing you to drop out. Your flight leaves on Saturday." As she stood up, I grabbed at her hand, but she shook me off. "I'd like you to go now."

"Wait." I couldn't catch my breath.

"What?"

"Will I see you again before I leave?"

She shook her head.

"So, this is it?"

"Yes," She tilted her head up.

I started to sweat. "Will I see you again, ever?" When she didn't reply, I opened the envelope. Between the pages of a brand-new passport was a one-way ticket to Seville.

# Soleá

Her name was Lola de Los Reyes and although I stayed with her for almost a year, I never really knew her. She was my mother's cousin, and I was sent to live with her when my mother, Lila, sold our house because I had unmade our family. Lola's home was in the old town of Seville, and every morning guitar notes, like flower petals falling, drizzled from blue-tiled balconies onto the cobblestones, and flamenco dilated into the streets, looping around corners to cross parks and plazas until it cursived itself throughout the city. Lola split her time between giving flamenco classes at Estudio Flamenco de Los Reyes, a flamenco school started by her guitarist father but was now run by her, and performing in the glitzy flamenco *tablaos* geared for tourists or dancing in the rundown *peñas* for herself. The *peñas* were clubs started by *aficionados*, so artists could improvise into the night as they continued learning, for true flamenco was music that had no end, and once it rubied your blood, you were set on a long road of patience.

The Estudio Flamenco de Los Reyes was located in the gypsy quarter near the Guadalquivir River, which carried the barest traces of the sea. Although there were many flamenco studios tucked behind corrugated metal doors or found up flights of stairs in gentrifying factory buildings, the Estudio Flamenco De Los Reyes was the most popular, partly because real flamenco was a family affair, and the de Los Reyes family was a family of great weight, but mostly because of Lola. Lola resided in the pulse of movement, and her myth had found root in flamenco. With her imperfect body full of strange, hard will, Lola danced her whole life, carrying sorrow and joy in the same step, turning. Colluding with flamenco's percussive layers of sound, her footsteps were raindrops, coming faster, multiplying, until her feet became summer lightning, and sound drowned out thought.

In the adhesive heat of rehearsal rooms, Lola kicked her heels so fast they'd blur, becoming the ghost ruffles of ocean white-caps, releasing a tidal wave of sound which pulled you in. Her sweat-slicked skin picked up stray light, powering the spotlight of her focus, where her students danced, sweat pearling their eyelashes, desperate to be seen. When a lesson finished and the studio emptied, the stilled room held the aftereffects of guitar melodies, clapped *compás*, heel stamps—remembrances of sound that reached back through the campfire of ancestry to echo ancient tales.

I arrived in the ambrosia twilight of late May, a sharp contrast to the cold, gray Detroit I had left behind. Cody, a friend of my mother's, had taken me to the airport, where I stared at every dark-haired woman in the check-in area with the hope that Lila might appear to say goodbye. Cody, as persuasive as broccoli, kept listing all the reasons why my new life in Seville was going to be better than my old life in Detroit as his eyes hopscotched from dark-haired woman to dark-haired woman too. Tension silly-stringed us together, looping around our necks, pulling tighter. After my bags were checked and my boarding pass was issued, I told Cody he would miss me before I gave him back his apartment key and joined the line at security, realizing that for the first time since second grade, I no longer had a key to any place to live. Being untethered was a feeling of clouds; patches of melancholy, gray and vague, giving way to prowling daggers of light. It was 2015, the year I sent my father back to prison, and Lila turned her back on me, the year my anger was a hunger. I was sixteen, aggrieved and adrenalized and adrift, balancing on the edge of something, my back against something else. Memories trespassed on the present: Lila with war in her eyes; Jesse, glassy-eyed and high; Cody's helpless, bovine eyes running over, so I stopped at a kiosk to look at postcards because nothing bad ever happened in postcards. When the memories dissolved into static, I could breathe.

Pulsating with intensity as though rhythm ran through her, Lola would have been easy to spot in the arrivals lounge among the hugging reunited even if she hadn't been holding a sign with my name on it because she still looked so much like Lila. Same sloe eyes, same dark hair swimming loose, spider legging her shoulders. When she spotted me, I split and watched us from the ceiling, I split and watch us from customs, I split and watched us from across the Atlantic and tried to see what she knew and what she thought of me if she knew. Her smile gave nothing.

"*Hola, mi querida.*" She kissed both my cheeks. "*Estoy muy feliz de tenerte aquí.*" Her words ran, sounding like language turned inside out.

"*Hola, tia Lola,*" my American accent flattened the inherent melody of spoken Spanish. Opening my mouth, I wanted to thank her for letting me stay, but all my high school Spanish had left me. My face heated.

"*Vale, vale. Venga.*" She took the handle of my smaller suitcase and wheeled it in front of her toward the exit doors where a line of white taxis stood, a row of small, even teeth, gleaming in the tangerine light. As the sliding glass doors pulled apart incompletely like parted lips, warm, citrus-scented air bathed my face. Several drivers scrambled out of their taxis to assist Lola with my suitcase despite the frenzy of travelers vying for rides. Lola opera-laughed as a driver opened her taxi cab door, wagging her ass into the back seat. Watching her get into the taxi was my first lesson in how movement could be an exclamation point, how everything around it could quiet and fade.

❧

Jaws wired shut by Spanish. Nodding shyly. Saying yes to every question. Mispronouncing words. Walking in the wrong direction. Walking into the men's bathroom. Getting lost in the maze of streets surrounding the cathedral. Retracing your steps in the Santa Cruz neighborhood over and over and over again, without realizing it. Forgetting where you locked up your Sevici bike. Forgetting where you lived. Forgetting your school uniform skirt. Not realizing a classmate standing on the first-floor stairway had taken photos from up your skirt. Not knowing what Podemos is. Not knowing what you think about Catalan independence. Not knowing who Princess Cristina is. Pretending to know about Franco. Not caring about football. Not caring about Eurovision. Buying hair sunscreen when you wanted hair conditioner. Not recognizing vegetables in the supermarket. Clucking like a chicken to a lunch counter server because you don't want meat. Not knowing the different cuts of ham. Taking a huge gulp of orange wine, expecting it to taste like orange juice, and coughing. Not knowing when to kneel in Mass. Not knowing how to say your prayers, in Spanish or in English. Getting into the communion line and helping yourself to a wafer. Saying *estoy embarazada* (I am pregnant) when you want to say, "I am embarrassed." Not knowing how to dance the *sevillanas*. Not knowing how to pin a *manton*. Stepping in the wrong direction in a dance line. Knocking into another dancer. Tangling your feet in a turn. Clapping on the wrong beat. Clapping the *palmas* hard when you should clap them soft. Not keeping your elbows back. Forgetting your dance shoes. Farting silent but deadly in a crowded dance class. Having loud, smelly, painful diarrhea in a dance studio bathroom. Bleeding on a borrowed rehearsal skirt. Re-watching *If I Stay* over and over again, all weekend long.

At some point, I caught on.

"¡*Eschucha*!" Lola was pounding the rhythm into the rehearsal room floor with a thick wooden stick. We paused, our ears registering the alternating hard and soft sounds of the *soleá*, the mother of all flamenco *palos*, its three, six, eight, ten, and twelve counts more heavily accented by the thud of Lola's stick. As her proud head nodded, her large hoop earrings bounced, deflecting from the years' inscription around her mouth, and the guitarist, Javi, began playing. His guitar notes, murmuring then lacy, were confetti all over the room, coating us in a protective layer as we danced until the room smelled of upheaval, and our bodies were filmed in sweat and dirt from creating a wall of sound. When the lesson ended, everyone clapped, a mutual applause for their endeavor to be like Lola, for every dancer in that room, no matter how much she gossiped about *la familia* de Los Reyes outside of the studio, longed to dance without hesitation like Lola, which was also how Lola lived. As we mopped the sweat collecting like quartz on our skin, Lola urged us to continue studying, saying Paco de Lucia had died learning, and he was *el padre de todo*. She encouraged us to go out into the streets, where we could improvise with other *flamencos* as we gave ourselves over to the *palos*. While everyone rushed off to change, I lingered, my body a sack of sand, and stared at the hundreds of framed, old photographs and charcoal pencil drawings crowded together on the studio walls. Most were of different members of the Reyes family—in which I saw traces of my own features among the faces of strangers—dancing, playing the guitar, singing in the *tabancos*, *peñas*, and *tablaos* of pre-gentrified Seville; others were posed portraits of famous flamenco *figuras*, stiff and regal in halted motion. In one photo, a dancing man in a tight black suit over a tight black shirt, its buttons straining over a slight bump of belly bulge, lifted his arms out of the frame. His chin length hair, slick with sweat, coiled around his hooked-nose face. In the corner of the photo, a girl, dressed in jeans and a white button-down over a T-shirt, clapped the *compás*, her head down, eyes glued to the dancer's feet. In another photo, probably taken the same day, the girl was turning, her arms forming a Z on either side of her torso, her white shirttails spreading like wings, her exuberant hair tied away from her face, skimming her butt. Looking at that photo made my blood run like lava through my veins, fueling hurt and longing. The photo was of Lila, about thirteen years old, her face unmasked, incandescent, dancing on a public stage, the words "Center" and below it, "Don," hanging on the wood-panel wall behind her. My eyes skidded to a drawing of an older man in profile, a curl of hair from his receding hairline drooping over his forehead toward his aquiline nose. My mind scanned through a mental gallery of artists who practiced regularly at the studio and landed on an older man, his belly bigger, his hair thinner and grayer, who sometimes joined Lola in a rehearsal room, accentuating the percussion of the *palmas* with a cane he beat onto the floor. I turned off the lights and exited, returning the rehearsal room to its austere, nonfunctional elements.

A staccato hit of heels fueled by adrenalized, fatal energy ricocheted from the studio next door. Inside, Lola was rehearsing, her arms circling her sides, the mechanism of a windup toy. I knew better than to interrupt, so I went into the changing room and grabbed my phone. I spent the next thirty minutes hunting for pictures of Lila on the studio walls and taking photos of them with my phone. When Lola took a break, I was ready for her.

"*Mi querida.*" Lola lifted her heavy hair from the base of her neck. "*¿Te gusto las clases de baile?*"

"*Sí, mucho.*" Holding the phone to Lola's face, I asked, "*¿Me puedes hablar de mi madre?*" A strange look crossed Lola's face, so I pointed to the picture of young Lila dancing on the stage, saying, "*Digame, por favor.*"

Lola's eyes turned me over, made me feel liquid. "*¿Te dirá qué?*"

What could she tell me? I puddled with questions. I wanted to know what Lila was like when she was young, before life had choked what was voluptuous from her. How she was when she was dancing and why she had never shared flamenco with me. I wanted to know if she regretted having me, if she ever asked about me, had she ever loved me. "*Todo.*" My heart struggled to hold it all. Then I asked her in patchwork Spanish why Lila stopped dancing.

"*Para bailar flamenco, necesitas ser trueno de corazón.*" Lola grabbed her phone and typed into a translator. "Thunder hearted?" She checked the phrase with me. When I nodded, she continued, "*Sentir la base de*—" she handed me her phone so I could read the screen. "To dance flamenco, you need to feel the ground of your life and the heart of the world." As I nodded, she added, "*Lila siente solamente la corazón de Jesse.*"

Jesse's heart for the heart of the world was a trade I would not have made.

❧

I heard she's American.

I heard she's from Detroit.

She's friends with Astrid now.

Did you see Señor Aguayo's pants?

I heard he's a perv.

I heard she's a slut.

Isn't Detroit like the murder capital of the world?

Did they ever find that guy who murdered the girl in the well?

My mom says she won't let me go to the *feria* this year.

What about that other dead girl?

Wait, there's another dead girl?

I heard a refugee did it.

Yeah, he had chalk all over the front of his pants.

Did she get suspended?

Bro, it was so funny! LMAO

Those Muslims. Look at what they just did in Paris.

He's up front, talking about photosynthesis, blah, blah blah, with a sugar-frosted nut sack!

Her parents are like real important. EU economic development, I think.

All the expats clique together.

Did you see those pictures Pepe took?

I thought I'd pee my pants.

*He* got suspended.

He's a local.

Girl needs to shave.

Señor Aguayo deserved it. He shouldn't rest his—himself
on the girls' desks.

Her aunt or cousin or whatever is a local.

I bet his parents are pissed.

Why isn't Señor Aguayo suspended?

Talk about friending up. Just because you're foreign.

All men science teachers are creeps.

I heard her aunt, cousin, whatever used to be some big
flamenco dancer.

Yeah, and Pepe's parents still have to pay the entire year's
tuition for him.

I heard she's failing.

I heard she failed out of her last school.

Those gypsies. They're always trouble.

This school is so corrupt.

Did you watch the FC Sevilla game?

Why would a grown-ass man want to work in a high
school?

Education is one long con.

Real Madrid all the way.

They should stay on their side of the river.

Bro, I can't wait for Christmas break.

So, wait. Did Astrid get suspended or didn't she?

Astrid can't dance.

What's up with Astrid's hair?

We're going skiing in the Pyrenees.

That new girl can dance.

᷎

I cut school and walked through the cold, needle rain pricking my face to La Macarena, a working-class neighborhood gentrifying into something it was never supposed to be. I went first to an old *taberna* where Lola's father, Roberto, sometimes played guitar. It was the kind of place which filled nightly with locals who looked sloppy and criminal but carried flamenco's breath and heartbeat inside them. A song would ignite, pulling passersby through the bar's wooden double doors or riveting them to the narrow sidewalk below the bar's open windows. Guitar notes lassoed the newcomers to the beer-flavored locals before the crack of a hard-soled heel split the air, or a voice, big-throated and agonized and plush, washed over them.

The cold damp followed me inside where an old man with a pastry-chef belly was wiping down the bar. He eyed my school uniform and then the clock on the wall and shook his head. *"No estamos abiertos."*

I assured him that I didn't want anything to drink and asked if it would be okay to take a look around as I skirted between pairs of green-painted, metal support poles covered in beer bottle labels, not waiting for his answer. I made my way toward the book-lined alcove, which was filled with well-thumbed Spanish paperbacks. Standing among spare kegs of Cruzcampo, I scanned the back wall, littered with sepia photographs and old *carteles* advertising local shows, my shoes sticking to the worn tiled floor. I shifted, and my shoes made a ripping, crackling sound, over which I coughed, aware that the man behind the bar was still watching me. I didn't find any pictures of Lila, but in the sea of black-and-white photos was an old Polaroid, its white border edges yellowed by cigarette smoke. In it, a man who looked like Roberto sat holding a baby, awe stretching his gray-stubbled cheeks, a guitar resting against the keg next to him. Leaning in close to take a photo of the picture, I lost my balance, falling into one of the kegs. *"Lo siento,"* I called over my shoulder as the old man came out from behind the bar, warning me to be careful. He joined me in front of the flamenco collage, his eyes skipping among photographs and framed bull fighting postcards, our shared privacy somehow reverent. He spoke first, pointing to a photograph of a man holding a pool cue as he lined up his shot and a young boy reaching for a billiard ball from the safety of his mother's arms. "*Yo*," he said as he pointed to the man shooting pool, sounding a bit surprised as if he couldn't understand what time had done to him.

"*¿Es tu hijo?*"

"*Sí*." Pride swelled the word, stretching it long.

I scrolled through my phone to the picture of young Lila dancing in her jeans and a white button down in front of the wood panel wall with only the words "Don" and "Center" visible before I offered him my phone. "*¿Sabe usted dónde está esto?*" I wanted to huddle up inside myself.

"*Sí, claro. Está muy cerca de aquí.*" He looked from the phone to my face. "*¿Es tu madre?*" He handed me back my phone.

"*Sí*." I felt like a broken doll on top of a trash heap.

Returning to the bar, he grabbed two glasses and filled them with dark liquid. Beside them, he placed a wooden cutting board and a knife and then reached inside a beer cooler and brought out some buttery, sock-smelling cheese, which he began slicing.

"*Me llamo Manuel.*"

I told Manuel my name was Lava and that I was happy to meet him.

He handed me a glass. "*Vino de naranja. Salud.*" He knocked his glass into mine and then drank.

I took a gulp of the orange wine and coughed. It was thicker and harsher than I thought it would be, a cross between Orange Crush and cough syrup. Manuel put an ice cube in my glass and told me to sip it. Then he gave me some cheese, which was nutty and made the wine taste more like honey.

"*Tu madre bailaba aquí cuando era joven.*"

"*¿Realamente?*" I couldn't picture Lila, ripened with youth, dancing here in the smoke and dirt, among the locals. "*¿Hay fotos?*"

Manuel threw up his hands and gestured to the walls. "*Me encanta verla bailar.*"

I nodded my head. I loved seeing her dance too, her private moment of breaking free from her corset of restrained living, but I was surprised he remembered it. I took a small step and moved my schoolgirl parts away from him.

"*¿Bailas?*"

I nodded my head, remembering my recent breakthrough, a moment of redemption or perhaps faith; I had danced by feeling the rhythm instead of counting it and finally started to express in the space between guitar notes. When Manuel asked me if I had fire as a dancer, my body glowed with aches. Fire was something I associated with Lola, but perhaps I had some too. I told him maybe.

"*¿Eres buena? Tu madre es muy buena.*"

"*¿Qué?*" This was too much because Lila didn't dance anymore. "*Mi madre ya no baila.*"

"*Sí. La vi bailar.*"

"*Mi madre vive en los Estado Unidos.*" My eyes ran liquescent. "*Se llama Lila Guajardo.*"

Manuel took away my glass of wine and replaced it with a bottle of water. "*Perdóname. Pensé tu madre es Lola de los Reyes.*"

When I explained that Lola was my mother's cousin, he looked at me in a way that made goosebumps flower on my skin. I decided to go. "*Gracias por el vino y el queso. Tengo que irme. ¿Dónde está?*" I pointed to the picture on my phone.

"*Centro Cultural Don Cecilio está aquí.*" He drew a quick map on a cocktail napkin.

"*Gracias.*" I grabbed the map and ran out into the bucketing gray.

The cultural center was located near the Basilica de Macarena, which housed the Virgin of Hope, so I decided to stop in for good luck. Between the restored Moorish city gate, now painted a Disney yellow, and the basilica was an old man, his hat pulled low over his head against the mahogany day, feeding baby pigeons—something you never see. Glistening fallen leaves, round like goldfish, pooled in the church courtyard's twiggy flower beds. I imagined the Guadalquivir, dark and oily like the man's hat, being frothed by the wind onto the river walk below Calle Betis, carrying dead leaves and debris out to the sea. Clouds of my exhalation diffused into the cold air as I watched the baby birds peck at the tiny pieces of bread which fell from the man's hand and wondered what had turned Lila away from her rhythmic story.

Anger bulleted my throat as I walked into the church and genuflected, dipping my hand into the holy water like Astrid had taught me. It must have been an off-peak time because the church was nearly empty except for a well-exercised woman who seemed like she had come in just to escape the rain. She was sitting in a backrow pew, checking messages on her phone. An old woman dressed in black and waddling like a penguin made her way to a stand of candles which smelled like brevity, lit one, and knelt, her lacey black veil obscuring her face. I slid into an out-of-the-way pew and knelt, watching to see if her veil would catch fire when it came at me on cat feet.

*Here you are. In second-day socks. With egg breath. You don't even know how to pray. You child of addiction. You father-jailer. Family wrecker. You Detroit city high school dropout. You flamenco wannabe. You child of a convict. You give away. You're airless and dark and cancerous. Your own mother won't tell you where she lives. You nowhere girl.*

My cheeks were wet as I knitted my fingers together under my chin and thought about the last time my hand and Lila's hand were still friends, but instead of talking to God, I breathed the regal, restrained heartbeat of the *farruca*. Red and blue clouds burst under my eyelids. In my head, I conjured the free fall of guitar music and let the notes gild me in the privileged language of flamenco. My body dilated under the thunder of percussion, swelling layers of memory into a dull casing. Realizing I had been looking for grace in the wrong house, I enforced composure and headed to the Don Cecilio Cultural Center.

The Don Cecilio Cultural Center had had an unhelpful makeover since Lila had danced there in her whirling Oxford shirt tails, her feet the hurt color of raw bacon. The bare wood panel wall backdropping the stage now featured two large, gold-framed generic flamenco dancer prints bookending either side of an ornate, oval shaped, gilded mirror. Outlining the backdrop were hanging tambourines painted with charming vistas of the pastel-colored houses lining the Guadalquivir. These were interspersed by large, decorative, black-lace hand fans. Lola scorned the use of fans, as she did castanets, saying they were shortcut accessories to mask unexpressive or lazy performances. Rain muttered on the rooftop as I slid onto one of the many wooden chairs set in rows before the stage. Manuel's confusion about Lola being my mother was stamping a 4/4 rhythm in my head when I had the prickly sensation of someone behind me.

*"Dígame."* The informal greeting was followed by a cigarette cough. I turned in my seat and eye-locked on an old woman whose attention felt like a warm current of witchcraft. Secrets whispered from the woodwork as she glided toward me. The red fringed shawl draped over her shoulders rendered her half madam, half high-priestess.

*"Me llamo Lava—"*

"I know who you are." Her voice was rich, dark, and resonant. As she lowered herself into a chair beside mine, I breathed in her velvet scent of tuberose and rum. A strong feeling of déjà vu washed over me.

"Do you know why I'm here?" I took in her penciled eyebrows, her fuchsia lips.

"Do you know why you're here?" Because she was sitting so close to me, when she spoke, my breastbone vibrated.

A long moment of mosquitos in my heart. "I want to know my mother." I opened my phone to the photo of young Lila dancing and offered it to the woman before me. She didn't glance at it.

"Then why are you here? If you want to know your mother, go home."

How to explain that I couldn't? "What's your name?"

"My name is Estrella." She said her name like it was cotton candy. "But that's not so important for what you want to know."

"How do you know my name?"

"I told you. I know who you are." She gave me a Mona Lisa smile. "If you want to know who you are, and you'll need to know yourself to really dance flamenco, then you should go home." With that, she lifted up from her chair and flitted away in her elegant trousers.

It was only as I put my key into Lola's front door that I realized Estrella had spoken to me in English.

๛

You knew before you knew although you took a lot for granted. Everyone around you was counting on you to take it all for granted. There were the ambiguous looks and confused apologies and dropped topics you didn't clock—all gobstoppered over the chalky, sour center everyone knew about but nobody spoke of. When you're blind, everything is on trust. But really, there is so little of it.

When you're older, you will know that all along the dark, hard part of you, the part that kept score, the part that instigated, the part that was a magnet for destruction, that part knew. That part had been right all along.

๛

I knew my breakthrough in flamenco was real when Lola invited me to join her at a new *peña* not far from the language school where I had taken Spanish lessons when I first arrived in Seville. Lola was performing with Javi, the guitarist who usually accompanied her at the school, and a singer from Cadiz. At the end of the show, I would join the artists on stage to clap the *palmas* for *el fin de la fiesta*, a short musical piece similar to an encore, meant to send the audience home in a festive mood, and if the feeling was right, Lola would issue a *llamada*, an invitation for me to dance. I thought about thirteen-year-old Lila, her eyes glued to the dancer's feet as she clapped. When I asked Lola if we could rehearse together, she scoffed, saying if I needed to rehearse, I wasn't ready, for true flamenco was created when players, knowing flamenco's structure, came together and improvised to share their experiences of living. She reminded me that dancing flamenco was not about practicing gestures and expressions, but rather it was a dialogue expressed through movement, and you didn't rehearse dialogue before you went out for the night with your friends. It was my job to study the structure, to know the intentions of flamenco steps and to know how those steps fit with different rhythms. That was why I should go to class every day and then go into *la calle* and dance with others; because the only way to really know another language was to speak it.

Walking through the swallow of the city to *peña* El Turruñelo, I passed by Bodeguita Fabiola, daring fate to show me Daniel, but the outdoor tables were as empty as the late January streets. There was no reason to justify going in, so I didn't. I had already given Daniel my virginity, which he wiped up with a tissue and let the wind take to the river; he didn't deserve anything else from me. Instead, I paused near an old church, conjuring the sententious tones of the *soleá* until I felt the waves of song on my skin tickle like dandelion petals under a chin, signifying a taste for butter. My body wound up as a tic tock of footsteps revved to a frenzy, trying to beat time, and then wound down. Now cleansed, I was ready to give myself over to the night's singing and dancing.

Many of Lola's students and some local *flamencos* were already seated around small tables enjoying beer and wine when I entered. I was surprised and not surprised to see Estrella nod her head and give me her Mona Lisa smile as I took a seat near the front and buzzed with anticipation. From some small back room came the syncopated thunder of heel stamps kickstarting a dancer's internal engine, underscored by a guitar being tuned. Javi came out first, took a chair and began playing, his hair falling in a comma across his forehead as his fingers danced over guitar strings, urgency pouring over melancholy. He slowed, allowing for a calm and silent moment before *el llanto*, the primordial cry of a singer, ushered a man with night-sky skin onto the stage. An indolent expanse of flesh flashed beneath his unbuttoned shirt as his voice, voltaic and vivid, pulled me a few inches from my seat, ar d my heart broadened. Images of Lila—asleep on her textbooks at the kitchen table, cutting apples in her nurse uniform for my lunch box, dancing flamenco on our linoleum floor—blinked on and off inside my head. The singer's voice, seeming to emanate from the earth itself, rinsed my anguish over Lila's abandonment, and for the first time, I regretted sabotaging Jesse's drug test. When the singer finished the *cante*, I was breathless and spent.

Javi's haunting *llamada* pulled Lola from the wings on a series of slow and deliberate backward steps. When I saw she was wearing trousers and a vest, my stomach tightened. She was going to dance the *farruca*, the *palo* I had studied all August to consume my longing for Daniel. Lola's arms rose to form an "L" as she crossed to the center of the stage and lowered as she spun as precisely as a drill bit on Cody's Makita. Her long arms carved smooth hieroglyphics in the air before her staccato feet sizzled the rhythm. Her arms became birds; sweeping, beating like wings, swirling on either side of her head before the rat-tat-tat-tat of her heels drew focus. As her heels stamped in quadruple time, they blurred with motion, and a channel opened through Lola to us, the audience, prickling our skin with the ax-edge of experience before an elusory power lifted us on a breath of wind and filled us with a primordial voltage—*duende*.

The audience exploded into applause, shouting ¡*Olé*! and ¡*Alé*! as Lola struck her final pose—her left hand lifted straight up in the air, triumphant, her right hand on her hip, insouciant—and continued clapping long after she had exited. By the time she returned to the stage, Javi had already invited me to join them. I stood on the far side of him clapping the *compás* as Lola returned to dance *el fin de la fiesta*, sweat still raining from her hair, rivering her face as her body lassoed. With my eyes glued to Lola's feet, I channeled my mother and let rhythm release me from myself as I alternated hard and soft claps to punctuate the tempo. When Lola closed a long section of footwork and issued the invitation for me to join her, my heart grew wings. Hearing Lola's *llamada* was an underwater feeling;

moving forward to dance was wading in a stream filled with slick stones. As I raised on my toes, arms lifting, fingers snapping, the audience and I took a collective breath, and I spoke my first true words of flamenco to Javi. He answered with his guitar, less a challenge and more a conspiracy, and together we celebrated life's chaos through the trigger of music. I danced a *mutis* off into the stage wings to generous applause.

I entered the dressing room on a rainbow, but no one was there to share it. The applause peaked as Lola took her final bow and then crested, soon replaced by the low rumble of conversation and a flamenco soundtrack. Lola entered the dressing room, smiling. "*Está guapo. Felicidades,*" she congratulated me and wiped at her streaky makeup with a towel while looking in the dressing room mirror.

"*Muchas gracias, por todo,*" I responded, watching her reflection. My reflection said to her reflection, Yes, I look like you. Maybe someday I will dance like you. Or better than you.

"*De nada.*" She was looking at me in the mirror, an almost twin, before she turned her attention to herself and removed the black pants glued to her legs.

I was averting my eyes when a little voice inside my head told me to look. Turning back to the mirror, I saw the five-inch scar below her belly button smiling above the lace of her panties. The realization was more and less than what I expected. "Lola?" My mouth tasted like chalk.

When she looked at me, both scarred and scared, I knew. A numb surprise.

I leveled her gaze back to her. "*¿Eres tu mi madre?*"

They're both suspended this time.

They cut school and posted some dumb pictures of themselves at the flea market.

Flea market? I bet it was the gypsy's idea.

I heard they're not friends anymore.

I heard she's a slut.

Real geniuses.

Astrid said she's a slut.

I heard she was busking near the Giralda.

Wait, are they or aren't they friends?

Did you see what was written in the girls' bathroom stall on
the second floor?

It's on, like, every bathroom wall.

She barely comes to school anymore.

Here, I took a picture of it.

They were friends but now they're not.

Señor Aguayo doesn't come to school anymore either.

Oh, man. You don't think? Naw!

LMAO.

Astrid said they're not friends because she's a slut.

I heard she was busking with some Black guy.

FC Sevilla killed it last night.

Wait, did Astrid get Señor Aguayo suspended?

Did your family get invited to a *caseta* for *feria*?

Did you get your dress for *feria*?

Is your mom letting you go to *feria*?

I can't believe that dead girl was almost a year ago.

The first dead girl.

I heard he took a sabbatical.

They're saying it's a sabbatical.

This school is so corrupt.

She said she's thinking about it if I text her every hour.

My grandmother's friend is sewing it.

Don't forget to have her add a pocket for your phone.

I heard Astrid's dad is getting her a dress from Angela y Adela.

Pepe's family has a *caseta*.

He says he's coming back here next term.

Must be nice. That store is so expensive.

We can go to his. They always have a lot of beer.

Get the shopping carts ready.

Is Astrid going?

Is the gypsy going?

You mean the slut.

Astrid still can't dance.

Gypsy, slut. Same thing.

I heard her family is invited to the mayor's *caseta*.

We'll have more fun at Pepe's.

Slut or no slut, Gypsy can dance.

# TARANTOS

Her name was Estrella Carmona, and in the end, I think I knew her. This was in Seville, where I was sent to finish growing up by the family I had grown out of. Estrella was a gypsy *cantaora* whose shattering voice evoked the lamentations of the black-smith forges from which her father came. Rivaling a *muezzin's* call, Estrella's voice, ecstatic yet plaintive, combined operatic intricacy and ethnic memory to cut or melt you, everywhere it touched, dripping. When she wasn't directing her waitstaff of handsome young men with a nod of her head or a whisk of a jeweled finger at the Don Cecilio Cultural Center, she sang the street opera that is flamenco. Sitting on a straight-back wooden chair on the bare stage, her vein-ridged hands delicately clasping and unclasping in syncopated claps, she would shut her eyes and set loose her voice, which echoed without limits on its wild runs, freeing the music living inside her.

Estrella sang the five-in-the-morning songs, the after-three-bottles-of-Carta-Blanca songs, the down-to-your-last-cigarette songs, giving bathos to the lyrics: *How joyous everyone is, and what a hard life I have; My glass is empty, I lost my way, I lost my way, mother* while keeping the pain real. The audience would laugh and then cry, their bodies trembling as Estrella brought them a sublime, shining closeness to death. It was her desolate, gypsy voice, with its trills and groans, which took me in when everything I thought I knew pressed up against everything I had yet to find out. It was 2016; I was seventeen and seeking family in the world of flamenco.

If you had a mother who had seduced a tourist for his dark skin and curls. If you had a mother who had seduced a tourist who also liked her cousin. If you had a mother who had seduced a tourist her cousin maybe loved. If you had a mother who had seduced a tourist who really loved his drugs.

If you had a mother who had seduced a tourist but really loved flamenco. If you had a mother who thought dancing flamenco was more important than being a mother. If you had a mother who was going to abort you until your father and her cousin offered to have you. If you had a mother who never intended to tell you the truth about your mother. If you had a mother who didn't ask for forgiveness. If you had a mother who didn't see you were worth more than she had decided, you might go looking for family too.

⊷

I stood in the eel dark outside the Don Cecilio Cultural Center, wishing I could disappear into a chalk outline of my own shadow. I should have been elated, having just danced my first public flamenco performance, but instead I felt a pain that was equal parts rage and grief. To her credit, Lola hadn't denied nor justified abandoned motherhood but offered up an olive branch of flamenco, saying its gypsy blood ran through both our veins, and that giving me flamenco was the best thing she could have ever done for me. I was cursing the valid novelty of my parentage when Estrella came outside with the alibi of a cigarette. Her eyes slow-circled my face.

I took in her enigmatic smile. "You were trying to tell me."

"I was." Estrella lit her cigarette.

"Why didn't you?"

"A person needs to discover her own interior cliffs." Her mouth broke open in a puff of pleasure as she blew smoke rings at the cobalt sky. "I gave you a necessary push."

"It gutted me."

"It opened you." Smoke rings haloed her head. "To be a conduit for flamenco, and that is what every singer, dancer, and guitar player is, you need to defy your limitations so you can channel flamenco's voltage." With her cigarette dangling between her lips, she began to clap the polymetry of the *soleá*, accenting the three, six, eight, ten, and twelve counts with a bump of her hip into my hip until I was clapping too. Taking the cigarette from her Mona Lisa mouth, Estrella sang: *I was a stone and lost my weight and rolled into the sea; And after a very long time, I came to find my weight again.* Under a fingernail moon, my back arched, and my arms swooped up and out, beating. My fingers became sea urchins above my head as I circled Estrella, and she sang: *I didn't mind; I know it was just a dream; Past things are in the past.*

"What were they like together?"

"Which two?" She smoked luxuriously. "Or did you mean all three?"

My face tarnished.

She threw me a look like she was sniffing something she might like to eat. "Don't be so shocked. This is flamenco."

I swallowed my naiveté. "Lola and Jesse. Lila and Jesse." I could barely wear my own face. "Lola and Lila. After."

"Are you sure? *Vale.* You will be the end of your own happiness." She took a final drag before throwing her cigarette to the ground. "Lola and Lila were more like two parts of a whole rather than two separate people. Only when they danced flamenco did they differentiate themselves, what with Lola having gypsy blood on both sides and Lila being raised in America. Lola understood the only way to know something was to live it, so she devoured flamenco. Really, she tried to eat it, take it into herself through every opening of her body. She left Roberto's house—"

"You know my grandfather?"

"Sevilla is a village, not a city."

"Why don't they speak?"

"Because of you. For a gypsy, family is everything. She broke his heart when she gave you away."

"Why doesn't he speak to me?"

"Because of shame and because he is loyal."

"How could she?" I paused to catch my breath. "Give me away?"

"The same way she could betray Lila by seducing the man Lila loved. Persecution is part of every gypsy's DNA. Combine that with flamenco, with its passion, its tragedy, its heartache.

It's *sentimientos fuertes*. All Lola ever wanted was flamenco. Giving you away fed her heartache, as did breaking Lila's heart, as did passion. It made her a much more riveting dancer. She also studied, practicing until her feet sweated blood—"

"What about Jesse? Why did he let her seduce him?"

"When Lola wants someone, the force of her desire is so strong that everyone and everything melt into nothing. And then her desire ends in the stammering pulses of orgasm."

I imagined Lola's messy fucking, and then her fucking boredom. "What about Lila?"

"What about her? She loved Jesse, so she let him have what he needed, which for a short time was both of them—"

"At the same time?" I had not yet learned that sex can dribble outside the lines.

"I told you, two parts of one whole. It wasn't supposed to have repercussions. Do you think it was easy for Lila to raise you? A constant reminder that despite giving Jesse everything, she wasn't enough."

I saw the leaky, faded hours when Lila ladled Jesse into bed, "Jesse's no saint."

"*Chica*, you have a lot to learn. Jesse is sick, not evil. He has been an addict most his life." Estrella muttered what could have been a curse or prayer under her breath. "For him, Lola was another drug."

I scowled at the night. "Do you know where Jesse is now?"

"Yes."

My skin porcupined. "And Lila?"

"Yes."

There was an instant freezing of my organs. "Could you tell her how sorry I am? Especially now that I know the truth?"

"She knows."

"You don't know that—or maybe you do, but if I could—" I felt like I was pedaling a bicycle backwards.

"You can't. You have already done. Sometimes, the best you can do for someone is to leave them alone."

⁌

I first met my mother watching her alchemize airport taxi drivers with the swing of her hips and the bounce in her breasts,
movements she took for granted but others were starved for.

I first met my mother in a dance studio, where I was baptized in sweat as she taught me my first words of her native
tongue, flamenco. As syllables are used to forms words; Lola
taught me the *chaflán* (foot slides), *golpe* (heel stamps), *latiguillo*
(toes scrapes), and *planta* (ball of the foot strikes) used to form
*pasos*, dance steps. I strung these movements into phrases, step
by step, to dance an *escobilla*, or the long footwork section of
a *palo*, building sentences out of phrases. Instead of counting
numbers, I counted the twelve beats of a flamenco *compás* and
learned how to use a *marcaje* to signal the rhythm to the guitarist.

I first met my mother on a rooftop where I watched her
dance to the music from her father's guitar, ignorant of my
ancestry. Her hips rocked back and forth, a heartbeat, before
they turned in one direction as her torso twisted in another.

I first met my mother watching her on a flamenco stage
after she answered the guitarist's *llamada*. She stood with her
back slanted at an impossible angle, her arms fluttering like
dove wings before her hands butterflied, freeing her fingers to
kaleidoscope the air. As the rhythm quickened, Lola's feet awak-
ened to stamp a manic heartbeat into the floor as if she were
tap dancing on tiptoes. She stilled, her diaphragm quivering
through her second skin dress, readying itself for the undula-
tions of her torso, which rolled like waves during low tide. Time
slowed as the column of Lola's body spiraled, the train of her
dress skimming the air, and reset when Lola's body halted, head
held high, back arched to the point of breaking, the dress train
wrapping itself around her legs like a lover begging her to stay
before she strutted off into the shadows.

I first met my mother in a dressing room mirror, where I saw
her C-section scar.

I first met my mother at the kitchen table the morning after
I realized she was my mother. We sat with our toast and cheese,

shying into our cups of *café con leche*, one person wanting something the other person was not ready to give.

I first met my mother in the other rooms of her trinity house, where I watched her mannerisms and catalogued her predilections for traces of my own. We both sat with our right leg crossed over our left but put our left shoes on first, cupped our hands over our eyebrows when we were reading, preferred to eat standing up rather than sitting down, liked mascara but not eyeliner, loved white chocolate but didn't like ice cream, picked at our cuticles, could snap loudly using our ring fingers, and had large feet but small ears.

I first met my mother standing at a bar, her dress purring her rump, as we shared midday *tapas*. I drank in how she arched the small of her back as her delicate hands rapped a flamenco *compás* on the wooden bar top, her hips rocking to the rhythm, drinks suddenly appearing for us. I tracked how her eyes magicked bartenders into giving us food we had not ordered or how her smile sometimes made our bills disappear, and I began to understand how Jesse and Lila did what they had done.

I first my mother watching her leave a key for the boy to whom I had given my virginity.

I first met my mother through an open crack of her bedroom door. She was sitting up in bed, her breasts hanging like deflated balloons, her hair flat and pasted to her skull, last night's makeup creased into the swells of her bloated face, bed sheets helter-skelter. From down the hallway and stairs came the sound of the front door closing.

Seeing and not believing. Imagining what I didn't see. Telling myself it didn't matter. Sitting at her kitchen table having coffee and milk, pretending it didn't matter. Knowing it wasn't her fault. Knowing it wasn't his fault. Blaming them both anyway. Pretending nothing had changed. Going to school and finding everything had changed. Eating her food. Taking my allowance. Borrowing her clothes and shoes. Taking her dance classes. Pounding my hurt and anger into the dance studio floor.

Feeling betrayed. Feeling too ashamed to talk about it. Class-mates talking about me. Astrid no longer talking to me. Eating lunch at a table alone, everyone around me talking. Scribbling out lies written on school bathroom walls. Going to the Don Cecilio Cultural Center more often. Going to the principal's office more often. Going to school less often. Going to flamenco shows. Spending my free time busking near the cathedral in a flea market flamenco dress. Finding more lies written on the bathroom walls, now with reviews. Going to classes at other flamenco schools. Not going to regular school anymore. Staying in Lola's trinity house less. Getting started when non-fla-mencos went to bed, greedy for the night. Nights with Estrella. Performing impromptu flamenco in the airless expanse of five a.m. Slipping on wet cobblestones. Dingy rooms. Throwing up in a *callejon* off the Alameda. Nights of nowhere. Not recogniz-ing my reflection in a mirror.

At some point, I settled down.

I got a part-time job at a rival dance studio in exchange for free classes, which I kept secret from Lola. I still studied with her, but it was hard for me to make sense of Lola, The Dancer I Wanted to Be Like and Lola, The Mother Who Had Given Me Away. The elusiveness of Lola was given full expression when she danced; her body sculpted air as longing scissored through her, and watching that, I understood her choice. Then Lola would dance a combination of violent and natural steps to close the *palo*, taking the soft white light with her, the moment evanescing, and I had to fight the propulsion to rush the stage and dance a death cusp, alternating strikes of heel and toe, stamping until I drowned in music. This was my *llamada*, which I knew she would never answer. For her part, Lola seemed unaffected, often commenting on my progress as my move-ments became more expressive and less mechanical although she did not invite me to dance with her again. She spent most of her time preparing for La Feria de Abril de Sevilla, having been hired to dance in a prominent politician's *caseta*, so when

Estrella suggested I join her at the *feria*, I jumped at the opportunity.

Since this was my first *feria*, Estrella insisted we do it right, as you should anything worth doing. On the evening of the fair's opening ceremony, I walked through streets water-colored with flowers, the heady scent of jasmine and orange blossom swirling through air salted with fried fish and the sun to Estrella's house to help her prepare a traditional *la cena del pescaito*. I loved going to Estrella's because her apartment building had such charm. Estrella lived in a remodeled *corrales de los vecinos* and in the interior courtyard of her building was a royal blue and canary yellow geometric-patterned tiled fountain, which I admired. The inner courtyard was dotted by lush, electric-green-colored plants potted in ornate ceramics, which had been made in the old gypsy factories just a few blocks away. A central staircase led up to a sidewalk of interior balconies which connected the private entrances of each apartment and created the feel of a small neighborhood inside the building. When I knocked on Estrella's door, she greeted me with a series of squeaky kisses on each cheek and a glass of *rebujito* to celebrate the beginning of the *feria*. Inside her apartment, the primitive roar of Camarón de la Isla, whose delicate, powerful voice could make your skin crackle, competed from a record player with the flat-footed heavy steps of tweens running in the apartment above us. Taking the thin-stemmed wine glass, I sipped the manzanilla sherry and 7UP mixture as I followed Estrella into her tiny kitchen, and the door snicked closed behind me.

Estrella washed her hands and gestured to the calamari, anchovies, and marinated dogfish laid out on wax paper on the counter. "Are you ready to get your hands dirty?"

Side by side, we rolled the fish in wheat flour before Estrella fried them in olive oil and sprinkled them with salt. Watching her turn the fish in the pan so it didn't burn while inhaling its buttery, cushiony smell made my heart meet my throat even as my mouth watered. When you are without a mother, you go looking in other people's kitchens.

"What?" Estrella eyed me as the fish sizzled.

I shook my head. "Nothing. Thanks for doing this."

"You will go out into the world many times and be bitten."

"That sounds like a T-shirt proverb."

"But the important thing is to go out again after you've bled." Estrella turned off her stove and set the fish onto a wad of paper towel to drain.

From somewhere in the building came the strum of a flamenco guitar. "It must be great to live in a building like this." I finished setting the table.

"It is. Will you get the pitcher of *rebujito* from the refrigerator? Less chaos than the old days, but a *corral* has always been a special place to live." Estrella brought the plate of fish to the table.

"Did you grow up in one?"

"I grew up here. When there was one bathroom for each floor and a communal kitchen."

"What? I never knew that. What was it like?" I refilled our glasses.

"Loud. *Corrales* were worker housing, for potters, sailors, bullfighters, and flamencos. Usually, you were related in some way to everyone in the building, which was both good and bad," Estrella laughed dirtily. "Instead of having your own apartment, you had a private room or two, so the courtyard became the center of social life, and in our *corral* there was always flamenco." Estrella knocked a 4/4 rhythm onto the tabletop and sang, "*Triana junto al arco de Triana. Triana junto al arco de Triana. Me voy a encontrar el amor mañana. Por la mañana.*" Finishing, she got up from the table and returned with an envelope which had a few loose black-and-white photographs. One showed a girl of about five, dancing solemnly against an old wall. In the foreground was a plain ceramic fountain, larger than the one I had passed in the courtyard, its sooty back wall decorated with a single crucifix. In the other, a boy was fighting a dog with goat horns tied to its head, bed sheets drying on a clothesline in the courtyard behind him.

"Omigod. Is that you? You're so serious."

"Thank God I grew out of that."

"Was that taken here?" I pointed to the fountain.

"The fountain used to be the main source of water for the *corral*. My mother and I were both baptized in it."

"No way!" I held up the picture of the dog and boy, giggling. "Is he pretending to be a bullfighter?"

Estrella's eyes were wet with laughter. "That poor dog."

"Is that your brother?"

"Cousin."

"Do you have more photos?"

"Photographs were for rich people." Some spittle flew out of her mouth as she coughed. "Nowadays, you kids with your selfies." But she was smiling. "I was very fortunate to be able to buy my apartment when the developers kicked the *gitanos* out."

"People were kicked out of their homes?"

"Yes. When the *payos* came in, they didn't like our gypsy ways, and they wanted our neighborhood. Sevilla was becoming more touristic and real estate was valuable. Non-gypsies have always had the power, so they drove up prices and drove us away."

"When was this?"

"It started in the '70s."

"Where did the gypsies go?"

"They were moved to a housing estate called Las Tres Mil Viviendas on the southern side of the city."

"Why haven't I heard of it?"

"You won't find it in the tour guides. Ugly tower blocks. Lots of crime, drugs, police guards. But our way of life survives, and it's where you'll find some of the rawest, most passionate flamenco. The dancer Farruquito is from there."

"Let's go! Can we visit?"

"*Chica*, it is the poorest neighbor in Spain, not just Sevilla. I have no desire to go there."

I thought about where I had grown up in Detroit, the faded-out smell of home. "Poor people don't scare me. We were poor in Detroit."

"And did you like it when people gawked at you because you were poor? When people don't have any money, we should let them have their dignity."

"That's not what I meant. I want to see how it is. I want…" I couldn't tell her I wanted to see how a family lives.

"I know." She patted my shoulder before she stood up and began clearing the table. "Let's clean this up and have a short nap before *el alumbrado*. If you play your cards right, you won't see a bed until sunup."

❧

Around eleven p.m. we left for the fairgrounds, walking along streets packed with people dressed for a wedding reception, men in suits and ties, ladies in silk or flamenco dresses, stumbling in their heels on the cobblestones toward the entrance to the fairgrounds to watch the lighting ceremony of the great arch. I was skeptical of the fuss. The one hundred and sixty-four-foot-high arch struck me as a cross between a Disney Magic Kingdom castle and a set piece from *Aladdin* until I saw its 22,000 light bulbs light up all at once. Estrella laughed at my gasp and grabbed my hand as we joined the amoeba of people engulfing the yellow sand streets under thousands of colorful paper lanterns, which were lit up as well.

The *feria* was huge: twenty-four blocks filled with rows upon rows of private *casetas*, individually decorated marquee tents, plus a bullring and an amusement park area with a big Ferris wheel and games to win giant, stuffed Minions. When I first heard about the *casetas*, I pictured burlap triangles planted in suburban backyards for summertime sleepovers, so I was unprepared for the gingerbread house roofs set atop red- or green-and-white-striped tent walls lined shoulder to shoulder on either side of the street. I felt like I had stepped into a Candy Land village. Because the *casetas* had to have their curtains pulled back during the lighting of the arch, I could hear and see inside several as we walked. Passing by them was like surfing the radio; constant waves of different kinds of music ranging from wailing flamenco to tinny Spanish pop were flowing out.

Most *casetas* had tables and chairs up front, a bar along the side with a kitchen behind it and a platform or dance floor in the back. The ritzier *casetas* had glass lanterns hung from the ceiling, mirrors, flamenco fans, floral arrangements, and colorful ceramic plates hung on the walls, potted fresh flowers staking the corners, and small, wooden tables and chairs painted with flowers in the front. I thought I saw Astrid sulking at a table with a fuchsia flower atop her head—dress, earrings, and lipstick to match—but I wasn't sure. It seemed like a lifetime ago since we had sung Adele together at the flea market instead of a matter of weeks.

"Where does this sand come from?" I was worried I'd ruin the shoes Lola had lent me.

"What does it remind you of?"

"I don't know." Sometimes, I just wanted a straight answer.

Estrella curled her index fingers atop either side of her head.

"The bullring?"

"Smart girl. It's called *albero*, and it's color is a symbol of Sevilla."

"What happened to your cousin, the one from the picture, who was bullfighting with the dog?"

"He sells auto insurance in Marbella. Come on, we go left here." Estrella kept a hand on my shoulder as she guided me to a modest tent toward the end of a row of *casetas* and nodded at the doorman as we walked inside. The red-and-white-striped walls were unadorned although the white ceiling was strung with red paper ball lanterns. Small tables surrounded by white plastic chairs crammed the entrance area giving way to a wooden platform backdropped by a large mural of a *corral de los vecinos* courtyard. Recordings of Paco de Lucia's fingers sizzling over guitar strings played above a constant rumble of conversation and sporadic clapping. Estrella pushed through crowd and the sand to plant me at a table near the front of the platform before disappearing and returning with a jug of *rebujito* and some plastic glasses. "Pace yourself. I don't want to have to wheel you home in a shopping cart."

"Does that really happen?"

"You'd be surprised."

"Where do the shopping carts come from?"

"How do you think the cooks get all the food here every night? Besides the horses and carriages, the *feria* is a pedestrian zone."

"What horse and carriages?"

"The *paseo de caballos*. It's the parade of horses and carriages that starts at noon every day. That's the best people watching of the *feria*."

"Why?"

"You'll see. I want something to nibble. Are you hungry?"

I shook my head, taking it all in, as Estrella left again for the bar. I wondered which *caseta* Lola was performing in that night, pictured her walking onto its platform in her street clothes and flamenco shoes and stamping short *golpes* onto various planks to test the acoustics. I pictured her changing into her flamenco clothes and wondered if she could have invited me to come with her after all. Estrella returned with a plastic plate of small green peppers cooked in olive oil and freckled with sea salt. A tall, leggy man with golf-ball cheek bones bobbled behind her. Estrella introduced him as Juan Fernández before he was pulled away by a group of *flamencas* to another table where he began to knock polyrhythms onto the table top for one of the women singing acapella.

"Who's that?"

"A dancer from Las Tres Mil Viviendas."

"No way." He didn't look like he lived in a ghetto tower. "He's tall for a dancer." Eyeing the speakers mounted on the upper corners of the tent, I asked Estrella what they were for because most shows I had seen were not miked.

Estrella regarded the speakers with regal impatience. "They'll play recordings of the *sevillanas* for people to dance to until the real music begins," she said and delicately slid a green pepper into her mouth. She scoffed at the pat structure of the *sevillanas* and got particularly annoyed if someone confused it for flamenco. As if she had conjured it, the *sevillanas* poured out from the speaker above.

"Music whisperer." I stood and offered my arm to Estrella. "Shall we?"

She sighed but stood, and we mounted the platform and faced each other with our opposite arms extended toward the sky as did several other couples. Alternating stepping closer to each other and then stepping away and punctuating these phrases with stylized turns, we danced each *paseo*, adding our own flourishes by way of intricate wrist turns and hip rocks, Estrella sometimes singing, our faces dramatically seductive during the *pasadas*. When the dance floor became too crowded, we returned to our table, which, too, had filled with people, some from the Don Cecilio Cultural Center, some faces I recognized from different flamenco classes, and a stray or two from Estrella's *corral*.

"Do you think Lola will show up tonight?"

"Sorry kiddo."

Someone shouted for the recording to be switched off, and the *sevillanas* was replaced by live guitar music coming from somewhere in the tent.

"Thank God." Estrella was happy to change the subject. "Now *la feria* has truly begun." She knocked her knuckles on the table top to augment the percussion of the *palo* while others sitting near us clapped the *palmas*. As I clapped, I thought about how I used to struggle to keep my hands relaxed enough to clap the muted sound of the *palmas sordes* or how my arms used to ache after *palmas* classes until I learned how to support my upper body with my torso. It had been nearly ten months since I had left Detroit, and for the first time, I owned my progress.

Chairs were turned and repositioned until most people were no longer sitting at separate tables but in a one giant, misshapen oval which took up nearly the entire *caseta* and allowed guitars to be passed from player to player more easily. When Juan Fernández took the guitar, Estrella sang "*Soleá de Triana*," everyone's mouths mirroring the lyrics, their eyes welling with tears. She finished to shouts of ¡*Ale*! and ¡*An otra*! above riotous clapping. She bowed in her chair, extending her arm to Juan Fernández and then out to the crowd to thank both him and the audience, and then asked him to continue playing because she wanted to see her good friend Lava dance. I turned to her; her face pleased with mischief. *Dance!* her eyebrows urged as breath shored into my lungs. There would be no dancing a little. It was all or nothing.

My voice shook as I asked Juan Fernández to play a *taranto* and set a steady 2/4 rhythm. *Tarantos* were usually used to convey sorrow and deprivation, but I heard the *palo* as more sensual. Needing a security blanket, I turned my back to most of the circle and kept my eye on Estrella, whose expression was pinned with encouragement. My hips rocked slowly and deliberately, alternating side to side and then out and around, the small of my back perking my butt out. It was something I had seen Lola do many times before she attacked a *letra*, slapping a *contratiempo* above her breasts and the tops of her thighs for maximum sound. I touched the top of each breast slowly with soft pats, lingering on my heart, then touched the tops of my hips, directing the audience's attention with flowing movement rather than cracking sound. My back arched in a fat C as I swirled slowly, imagining my body as a piece of licorice being twisted, arms forming a horizontal S on either side of my torso before I elongated, standing into the full frame of myself, my fingers feathering before my leg popped under my skirt so I could catch the hem and show my ankles and calves as I danced a *desplante*. Turning my back to the audience, my legs bowing into a cello, I again wagged my hips and ass to the strong, steady tempo before I danced a *cierre* to close the *palo*. Under the applause, I summoned Lola's feral, gypsy blood through my dotted outline of limitation and whispered to Juan Fernández, "*Esto es para ti.*"

This is for you.

❧

According to Estrella, Wednesday was the main day of the *feria*,

so after my work shift, I went home to quickly change, and then
I picked her up so we could go to the fairgrounds to watch the
*paseo de caballos* together. Lingering in her building's courtyard,
fragrant with citrus, I was admiring the colorful pottery hanging
on the walls near the entry arch when the memory of rhythmic
clapping echoed around me. Back arching, head tilting back, my
arms rose before I broke the voluptuous stillness with a chaos
of movement, and the sun cut the courtyard into angles of
light. The world blackened to pinpricks, time elastic, and there
was Juan Fernández, me pinning the four corners of his body
to a wall, the music drowsing us, my body boneless as it twisted
and curved in a three-dimensional plane, the dance storying all
over us, my body inchworming. Spent, I unfolded myself and
shivered with recognition, steadying my breath to the measured
heartbeat of the *corral*.

❦

"Chica, have I got a surprise for you." Estrella called from inside
her door. To a syncopated *pah, pa-pa-pah*, she slowly revealed
herself in the doorway.

"You look great!" Her gray-white hair glittered with rhinestones from hair combs nesting in her elaborate updo. A
violet cloth flower anchored behind her left ear matched the
cloth bougainvillea earrings hanging from her delicate lobes.
Her bell-sleeved flamenco dress sported tiers of sea foam and
minty green chiffon from the mid-thigh down, which gave the
impression she was floating when she walked. A jade and pink
flowered *mantoncillo* with violet fringe draped low on her shoulders, revealing the pale skin of her back.

"Thank you, but this is not your surprise. First, we must get
you ready."

"I am ready." I had walked over to her apartment in my flea
market flamenco dress and a castoff pair of Lola's shoes.

"You are dressed, but you are not ready." She guided me into
her tiny bathroom and sat me down on the closed toilet seat,
where she made up my eyes and pinned my hair into a low bun
decorated with gold leaf hair combs. Along the sides of my

head, she slid rhinestone bobby pins to catch the light. Atop my head, she planted a single huge red flower before she colored my mouth in a bold lipstick to match. When she was finished, she slid the lipstick tube into the cleavage of my dress and told me to pick a pair of earrings from the tin canister balancing on the sink.

"Why isn't your flower on top of your head?" I fished out a pair of blue chandelier earrings to match my dress.

"Because I am not a lovely, young and single lady." She disappeared into her bedroom and returned with a red embroidered *manton*, which she tucked and pinned into the back of my dress and fastened softly around my breasts with a bright blue stone brooch.

"This brooch was my mother's." She stepped back in appraisal and shook her head. Removing the pin, she took both ends of the *manton* and pulled tighter, pushing up my bosom. As she re-pinned the shawl, my eye was drawn to her earring, and my mind reeled to the contents of Lila's secret box. I caught my breath. "Estrella, are we related?"

"No, *chica*, but through our gypsy hearts, we are family." She stood me up and brought me to the mirror. "So?"

Looking at my reflection felt like pressing on a bruise, totems of both Lola and Lila in my grown-up features. With my hair pulled back and my face dramatically made up, I seemed much older than my seventeen years. The *manton* was big enough to cover the small stains and other signs of wear on my dress while still enhancing my figure. The total effect was that I looked like someone I might become, someone who had been out into the world and understood how it spun.

Estrella hadn't exaggerated when she said the *paseo de caballos* was premier people watching. Men—dressed in short jackets, tight trousers, riding boots, and wide-brimmed *cordobes* pulled low over their heads, banditing their eyes in shadow—sat next to women in flamenco finery inside open-top carriages painted to match the red and yellow paper lanterns hanging above the streets. Some people rode on horseback, and the horses had been decked out too, their faces wrapped in garlands of red and yellow ornaments.

"Be careful not to step in horseshit." Estrella held on to my arm as we walked alongside a row of *casetas*, dusting up yellow sand which smelled of sun-roasted dung.

"I will." But I wasn't. When I wasn't looking inside the *casetas*, I was admiring different flamenco dresses and wondering if the women who wore them could dance flamenco well. From farther down the street came a burst of applause, and moments later, a rider on horseback with Lola sitting sidesaddle behind him approached us. I had never seen a flamenco dress like hers; a one shoulder style, which reminded me of ancient Rome, purplish-gray and gleaming in the sunlight. The one sleeve was long and fell in a cascade of ruffles trimmed in black lace as were the tiers of ruffles on her skirt. Her long black hair, half up, half down, serpented along her naked shoulder, down her bare arm. "Lola!" I jumped up and down, waving, then strained for another look as she passed by. "Did you see her?" That vision of Lola deserved its own *palo*. "Do you think she saw us?"

"Probably not. Come on, or we will be late for your surprise." Estrella crossed the street and stopped in front of a black carriage with white-painted wheels pulled by two black horses with white hooves, which made the horses look like they were wearing gym socks. After she greeted the drivers, she turned to me and asked me if I had my phone.

"Sure." I tapped one of the layers of my skirt which had a pocket sewn beneath it.

"Good. You might want to take a selfie. Care to join me?" She extended her arm and swept it toward the carriage.

Planting a big kiss on her cheek, I hiked up my dress and climbed in. Estrella lifted the hem of her dress and followed. After we had settled and mugged for our selfies, she told the driver to avoid Calle del Infierno, where the amusement park was, and drive.

"I can't believe how many people are here." Looking around, I thought I saw Señor Aguayo leading a young girl by her arm away from the *caseta municipal*, but when I looked again, they were gone. A group of teens drinking bottles of beer around a plastic trash bag filled with ice caught my eye. I looked for Daniel's golden curls among the football huddle of heads but didn't find them.

"It gets more crowded at the weekend when people from other cities come."

"People don't seem to use the *casetas*. It's a shame they are private."

"They'll go inside once it gets dark. The *casetas* have to close their curtains around eight p.m. after the *paseo de caballos*, and people stay inside drinking and dancing."

"I can't picture these streets being empty." I stuck my hand out of the carriage, letting the breeze run between my fingers, buoying them aloft, remembering the dead girl found floating in a well, lost in the festivities of last year's *feria*. I imagined her being taken against her will, struggling in the desolate street, her cries for help drowned out by the *casetas'* revelry. "Is that why no one saw anything when that girl disappeared last year?"

"No one was looking. That kind of thing never happens, so when it did, it was easy for the *payos* to blame the gypsies when they couldn't find who had done it." Estrella looked like she wanted to spit.

Clouds blindfolded the sun. "That shade feels good. I am sweating in this dress." I wiped at my forehead, anxious to change the subject.

"They think we don't belong here when flamenco came from us, is us. It's our spirit, our suffering, our longing as we were driven from our homeland."

"I am sorry Estrella. I didn't mean to upset you."

"Why *chica*? My fire is proof I am alive. I live. The *payos*, with their costumes and fancy *casetas*, are playing at flamenco just like they play at being alive. There is no *duende* in their music, in their dance. There is no world's heart in their songs." This time she did spit. "Flamenco is a way of life, and these *payos*, they don't know how to live."

We got out of the carriage at the Triana *caseta*, where most of Estrella's friends had already gathered. They were starting to become my friends too, as I lived less in a teenage world of high school and homecoming dances and more in the world of flamenco, which ignored the rules that kept society civilized. I got greedy for the hours when non-flamencos went to bed, when I lived in the present with my whole body, rebuilding wreckage from a tangle of limbs and a syncopation of footsteps, as a *tocadore* played a *palo* from the inside out. Flamenco was a voice as vivid as the red licks leaping from old bullfighting posters, a voice that could draw you back to your first anguish and then abandon you in your own wilderness of memory. Flamenco was a conversation, a heart sharing of life's suffering and happiness, an outpouring of urgency over melancholy when life zigzagged. Flamenco was a life without architecture, but within the sometimes-scalding chaos, so often violent in its intimacy, a dancer sculpted space, emotion matching movement matching moment, a moment of bruised grace, of sweaty reprieve.

# GLOSSARY

*listed in alphabetical order*

*a palo seco* — to perform without accompaniment

*aficionados* — flamenco enthusiasts

*agua* — literal meaning is water; an exclamation of approval or encouragement

*albaceria(s)* — traditionally a grocery store; a bar selling wine, cuts of meat, cheese, and other small plates

*albero* — the yellow sand found in bullrings

*alé* — an exclamation of approval or encouragement

*an otra* — another

*bachillerato* — a highly academic two-year program prepping students for university studies

*bailas?* — do you dance?

*barrio* — neighborhood

*bodeguita* — a small bar selling wine and usually small plates of food

*braceos* — arm movements

*bulería* — a spirited song and dance from Jerez, with a fast, lively rhythm

*café con leche* — coffee with milk

*Calle del Infierno* — Hell Street; calle means street. It is a street at the Seville Fair.

*callejon(es)* — small side street

*campo* — the countryside

*caña* — a small glass of beer

*canción* — a song

*cantaora* — a female singer

*cante* — a song

*cartel(es)* — a poster

*caseta(s)* — a small house; at the Seville Fair, they refer to tents, either simple, opulent, private or public.

*caseta municipal* — a small house opened to the public at the fair

*chaflán* — a two-part step; stand on one leg, shunt yourself along the floor and then stamp with the other foot *chica* — girl

*cierre* — the end of a series of dance steps or a song

*claro que sí* — of course, yes

*codos hacia afuera* — elbows out

*colegio* — high school

*compás* — the beat, rhythm, or measure of a song

*contratiempo* — against time

*cordobés* — a wide-brimmed man's hat with a flat top

*corrales de los veinos* — worker housing; characterized by a large patio in
      the center which has a fountain or well to supply water

*danzaora* — female dancer

*de nada* — you're welcome

*desplante(s)* — a section of a dance

*dígame* — tell me

*dígame, por favor* — tell me, please

*doble tiempo* — double time

*Donde está?* — Where is it?

*duende* — the inner force or soul that inspires flamenco

*el alumbrado* — the lighting ceremony of the main gate at the
      entrance of the Seville Fair

*el fin de la fiesta* — the end of the party

*el llanto* — a cry

*el padre de todo* — the father of all

*Ella está muerta* — She is dead.

*empapado en música* — drenched in music

*en la calle* — in the street

*Eres buena? Tu madre es muy buena.* — Are you good? (meaning, do you
      dance flamenco well?) Your mother is very good.

*Eres tu mi madre?* — Are you my mother?

*es muerta* — to be dead; incorrect use of the verb "to be."

*Es tu hijo?* — Is he your son?

*Es tu madre?* — Is she your mother?

*escobillas* — a broom; in flamenco, a section of a dance with extended
      footwork

*Está aqui* — It is here

*Está guapo* — It is good; guapo can also mean handsome

*está muerta* — she is dead; correct use of the verb "to be"

*Estamos abiertos.* — We're closed.

*Esto es para ti.* — This is for you.

*Estoy muy feliz de tenerte aqui.* — I am very happy that you are here.

*falseta* — a melodic variation played by the guitarist

*fandangos* — a high-spirited dance for couples that has a
      triple meter

*farruca* — a dance traditionally performed by men with aggressive
      footwork and dramatic shifts in tempo

*felicidades* — congratulations

*feo* — ugly

*feria* — fair

*figuras* — star performers

*flamencas* — female flamenco performers

*Flamenco es fuerte.* — Flamenco is strong.

*flamencos* — male or a mix of male and female flamenco performers

*gitano* — gypsy

*golpe* — heel stamps

*Gracias* — Thank you.

*Gracias por el vino y el queso.* — Thank you for the wine and cheese.

*guajira* — a flamenco style influenced by Cuban rhythms

*Hay fotos?* — Are there photographs?

*He hecho una amiga* — I have made a friend.

*Hola, mi querida* — Hello, my dear one

*Juega para mi, Papá.* — Play for me, Father.

*la calle* — the street

*la cena del pescaito* — a fish dinner traditionally served during the fair

*la familia* — the family

*La Feria de Abril de Sevilla* — Seville's April Fair

*La vi bailar* — I saw her dance.

*Las Tres Mil Viviendas* — The 3,000 Homes, a poor neigborhood in
      Seville

*latiguillo* — toe scrapes

*letra* — a verse of a song

*Lila siente solamente la corazón de Jesse.* — Lila feels only the heart of
      Jesse.

*llamada* — a call; an invitation to join a dance; it signals the start of or
      a change in a section of a dance

*Lo siento.* — I am sorry.

*manton* — an embroidered silk shawl with long fringe

*mantoncillo* — a smaller, lighter version of a manton

*marcaje* — a marking; refers to the marking of beats in a rhythmic cycle by the dancer

*Me encanta verla bailar.* — I love seeing her dance.

*Me llamo Lava.* — My name is Lava.

*Me llamo Manuel.* — My name is Manuel.

*Me puedes hablar de mi madre?* — Can you tell me about my mother?

*Me voy a encontrar el amor mañana.* — I am going to find love tomorrow.

*Me voy convirtiendo* — I am becoming

*Mi madre vive en los Estados Unidos.* — My mother lives in the United States.

*Mi madre ya no baila.* — My mother does not dance anymore.

*mi querida* — my dear

*muchas gracias por todo* — thank you very much for everything

*muezzin* — a man who calls Muslims to prayer from the minaret of the mosque

*mutis* — to make an exit; the ending of a dance off stage

*olé* — an exclamation of approval, encouragement

*palmas* — the handclapping used to accompany flamenco singing or dancing

*palmas sordes* — muted or soft palmas done by hitting the cupped palms together

*palo(s)* — a flamenco rhythm or style of singing, also called a cante

*Para bailar flamenco, necesistas ser trueno de corazón.* — In order to dance flamenco, you need to be thunder-hearted.

*para carteles y cantos y palmas* — for posters and songs and clapping

*pasada(s)* — the act of passing a partner during the course of a dance

*paseo* — a walk; in a dance, it is a graceful part of a dance

*paseo de caballos* — the horse and carriage parade at the fair

*paso(s)* — a step in a dance

*peña(s)* — a club of flamenco aficionados

*Pensé tu madre es Lola de los Reyes.* — I thought your mother is Lola de los Reyes.

*perdóname* — pardon me

*planta* — the sole of the foot; the movement of striking the flat of the foot against the floor

*Podemos* — a left-wing, populist party favoring anti-austerity, anti-corruption, and anti-establishment

*Por la mañana* — in the morning

*punta* — point, the striking of the tip or toe of the shoe against the floor

*Que?* — What?

*Realamente?* — Really?

*rebujito* — an Andalusian cocktail of sherry wine and lemonade or lemon-lime soda

*remate* — to finish off, to complete a dance sequence

*Sabe usted dónde está esto?* — Do you know where this is?

*salud* — cheers

*scheisse* — German for shit

*Se llama Lila Guajardo.* — Her name is Lila Guajardo.

*sentimientos fuertes* — strong feelings

*sentir la base de* — to feel the base of

*Sevici* — a bike rental company in Seville

*Sevillana* — a female from Seville

*sevillanas* — a popular festive folkloric Andalusia dance

*Sevillanos* — men and women living in Seville

*si* — yes

*Si, claro. Está muy cerca de aqui.* — Yes, of course. It is very close to here.

*siesta* — a short nap

*siquiriyas* — songs which express anger or despair

*soleá* — a form of song which is considered to be the mother of all flamenco

*soleá de Triana* — a soleá from Triana

*subidas* — a step in flamenco used to increase the speed of the dance

*tabanco(s)* — a partial tavern and wine shop that sometimes sells food

*taberna(s)* — a tavern with a bar and public rooms

*tablao(s)* — a flamenco nightclub

*tacón* — the heel; the striking of the heel against the floor

*taconeo* — heelwork; sometimes used to refer to any footwork

*taller* — a workshop; a dance workshop or school

*tangos* — the oldest flamenco song form which has a 2/4 time rhythm *tapa de tortilla Española* — a small plate of Spanish omelet

*tapas* — small plates of food

*tarantos* — a free-form style of flamenco

*Te dirá que?* — What shall I tell you?

*Te gusto las clases de baile?* — Do you like the dance classes?

*Tengo que irme.* — I have to leave.

*Tierra, trágame* — Earth, swallow me.

*tocadore* — guitar player

*todo* — all

*Triana junto al arco de Triana* — Triana, next to the arch of Triana

*Tú estas tarde* — You are late.

*Tu madre bailaba aqui cuando era joven.* — Your mother danced here
    when she was young.

*vale* — okay

*venga* — come

*vino de naranja* — orange wine

*volvimos* — we return

*Yo* — I

*Yo soy* — I am

*zapateados* — footwork; the striking of different surfaces of the foot
    against the floor

# ACKNOWLEDGMENTS

There are so many people who shared their stories and themselves, which helped create *Duende*: The Guajardo family, who brought me to my first *feria*, and whose warmth and love is contagious and bountiful; legendary guitarist Roberto Reyes, who taught me so much about life and flamenco, including how to clap a *compás*; Jose, Carmen, Murat, and Eva for answering my many questions about flamenco when I was not sure which direction this story would take; Lola, who opened her beautiful home to me and inspired Lola's home in the story; Pepe for showing me his Sevilla and Trebujena; and Angela and Adela, for dressing me up in their *Vogue*-worthy flamenco dresses.

Thanks to Karen Emslie for her critiques as I was writing this novella.

Thank you, Mom and Dad, for all I have done started with you.

Three institutions have supported me in the creation of *Duende*. Thank you to Can Serrat and Duplo A.I.R. by Linea de Costa for their artist-in-residency grants, which afforded me a place to research, write, and be inspired, and to the American University of Iraq, Sulaimani, which provided monetary support for these residencies.

Finally, I want to thank Sevilla, which has delighted and charmed me since my first visit in 2015, and flamenco, which always captivates. To quote one of my mentors and heroes, Jere Van Dyk, "Do what you love and then write about it."